**Dark of the moon,**
**hear our plea!**

*We ask for a father! A man to marry our mother!*

Caroline's shriek split the moonless night of the summer solstice. She clutched Ryan and pointed where the fog was thickest. From the gray, ominous mist emerged a figure. "It's a ghost!"

The man was tall, black-clad, with dark hair and eyes—like a modern-day vampire—and he was coming toward them. "I see fangs!" Ryan exclaimed.

"Maybe he eats kids," Caroline managed.

"That's only in fairy tales," Ryan scoffed.

"It's past the witching hour," the man finally said, keeping his distance. "Your mother must be frantic."

"Are you magic?" Ryan challenged.

The man stared at the children. He suddenly smiled. They wanted a father . . . badly enough to cast spells in a haunted meadow in Salem. "Maybe so, son," he said. After he met their mother, he'd let her decide.

Dear Reader,

It's no "trick"! Linda Randall Wisdom has a real "treat" in store for you with *Under His Spell,* the October Calendar of Romance Halloween title. It's delightfully funny . . . and wickedly sexy.

Next month, start to *Count Your Blessings* (#461) with Kathy Clark's special Thanksgiving romance.

We hope you're enjoying all the Calendar of Romance books. They're a great way to relive all the precious moments throughout the year.

We welcome your comments. Write to us at the address below.

Sincerely,

Debra Matteucci
Senior Editor & Editorial Coordinator
Harlequin Books
300 East 42nd St., 6th floor
New York, NY 10017

# LINDA RANDALL WISDOM

# UNDER HIS SPELL

*Harlequin Books*

TORONTO • NEW YORK • LONDON
AMSTERDAM • PARIS • SYDNEY • HAMBURG
STOCKHOLM • ATHENS • TOKYO • MILAN
MADRID • WARSAW • BUDAPEST • AUCKLAND

Published October 1992

ISBN 0-373-16457-2

UNDER HIS SPELL



Printed in U.S.A.

# *Prologue*

"Dark of the moon, hear us now, come to our aid and grant our plea."

"That's not a spell! Spells have words that sound the same. Everybody knows that," Ryan Bennett protested.

"Is so a spell. It's written right here in this book. And I have to say all the words before I put out the pictures you gave me."

"Is not a spell!" The little boy glared at the youth standing in the middle of a white circle roughly chalked in the dew-kissed grass. "We want our three dollars back, Kevin Elliott. You lied and cheated. You don't know how to make us a dad from magic."

"Come on, Ryan, if Mom finds out we're not in bed, we'll be in big trouble. Let's forget this," red-haired Caroline Bennett whispered, looking around the meadow fearfully, as if evil ghosts might suddenly appear and spirit them off. She grabbed her brother's arm and tried to pull him away, but he shrugged her off.

"Not till Kevin gives us our money back," he insisted, his squared-off chin jutting out stubbornly. He sneered at the other boy. "We shoulda gone to someone who knew how to conjure up a dad for us. Someone *smart.*"

"I know what to do," Kevin argued, holding up a large book with faded gold lettering across its well-worn, water-stained black cloth cover. "Mom's books are authentic witchcraft guides. If you do the spells right, you'll get what you asked for. So let me say the damn words, put the pictures in the circle and you'll get your dad!" he shouted.

"You're not supposed to say the *D* word," Caroline reminded him, her fear forgotten for the moment. "Your mom said if she caught you cursing again, she'd wash out your mouth with soap."

Kevin took advantage of his greater height and peered into his next-door neighbor's tiny face. "Well, Mom's not here, and I don't think you're gonna snitch on me, since you'd have to tell her where you heard me say *damn*, and then she'd tell *your* mom where you were tonight." That foolproof reasoning established, he challenged, "So, do you want me to get on with this or not?"

"I want to go home," Caroline whimpered, looking over her shoulder.

"I want a dad!" Ryan wailed, clenching his tiny fists. "A dad who will love us and Mom and not that dumb Eileen Butkus. I want a dad so I can get into Little League when I'm bigger and so he'll talk Mom into letting us have a puppy." He stomped around the white circle. "I want a dad who will live with us and make Mom happy!" He glared at Kevin as if it was all his fault. "But you can't do it, so I want our three dollars back."

"Ryan, we'd better get home!" Caroline moaned, continuing to look over her shoulder but unable to see much even with the full moon. She was convinced someone was watching them. Even more unnerving was the fog suddenly drifting across the grass. "I wish I'd never agreed to go along with this." She pulled on her younger brother's shoulder again.

Kevin, refusing to be deterred, stood in the middle of the circle and carefully placed the book at his feet, holding it open with the toes of his combat boots. He studied the pages again, glad he'd looked over the spell before coming out here. The words *were* kind of funny. Nodding with satisfaction, he straightened up and raised his arms, his fingers wiggling madly. Dressed in camouflage pants and a khaki T-shirt, with black-and-khaki camouflage paint smeared across his face, he considered himself an eminently appropriate sorcerer. "Dark of the moon, hear us now, come to our aid and grant our plea. These children ask for a man to be their father, to be there in their time of need, to love their mother and—"

"And give us a puppy!" Ryan shouted at the sky.

Kevin shot him a look fit to kill. "Whose spell is this, anyway?" he hissed. "Just let me do my thing, okay?" He took a deep breath and raised his face, his eyes closed as he continued to chant, "To love their mother and give them all they desire. So that the spirits might know what these children ask for, we offer up these pictures." He pointed to the ground.

Ryan immediately squatted and carefully arranged several magazine photographs of male models—and a picture of several puppies playing.

Kevin groaned. "What is it with these puppies?"

"I want one," Ryan insisted. "I figure if we can get a dad, we should be able to get one who likes dogs."

Caroline was past listening as, with wide-eyed fascination, she stared at the tendrils of fog snaking around Kevin's ankles. "Look," she whispered to her brother, gesturing toward the ghostly fingers of fog.

Ryan's bravado began to dissipate as he watched the mist drift up Kevin's legs. He stamped his foot. "Now I know he's doing it all wrong," he scoffed. "We should have that fog around us, not him. Now he's gonna get the dad meant for us! Kevin's so dumb!"

Caroline's shriek split the summer night. "Look!" she cried out, pointing where the fog was the thickest. From out of the ominous gray mist emerged a tall, dark figure—and the figure was walking toward them!

Kevin took one look, uttered a pithy curse, grabbed his bike and bolted out of sight.

"It's a ghost!" Caroline's lips quivered with fear. She stood frozen in place, and Ryan, beside her, was likewise too frightened to move. "It's going to eat us, and we'll never see Mom again."

"I see his fangs." Ryan couldn't keep his eyes off the masculine figure approaching them with ground-eating strides. "And his eyes are glowing red. Kevin didn't give us a dad. He used the wrong spell and made up a devil instead." He sounded angrier at Kevin for messing up the spell than terrified at the idea of being attacked by a demon.

Caroline grabbed her younger brother's hand and held on tightly, her lips moving with every prayer she could remember.

"Shouldn't you kids be home in bed?" The man stopped a short distance from them. His deep baritone emerged from the encroaching fog. His dark gaze took in the drawn circle, the antique book lying abandoned in the middle, and the two children frozen like statues.

"Are you gonna eat us?" Ryan asked, curiosity overtaking fear.

The man smiled. "No, son, I'm not going to eat you, but I do think you should get on home. It's past midnight. Your mother must be frantic."

Caroline took an experimental step backward, and when she discovered she could move, after all, she took another step. She pulled on her brother's hand.

The man carefully kept his distance. "You were probably taught not to speak to strangers and such, but I have an idea it's a long way home for you. Would you trust me to drive you?" He suspected he was pressing them to go against parental dictates, but he also knew he couldn't leave the tykes alone in the meadow in the middle of the night.

Ryan studied the man. Tall, with dark hair and eyes, dressed in a lightweight black sweater and jeans, he looked like a modern-day vampire. And vampires drank blood! Still, he didn't jump on them with his fangs bared, and he had a nice voice and smile. Could Kevin have said the spell right after all, and this man was going to be their dad? Hope sprang up in his tiny chest.

"He won't hurt us, Caro," Ryan whispered, his decision made.

She wasn't as trusting. "Mom said we're not supposed to talk to anyone we don't know or ever get in a stranger's car. Maybe he eats kids," she whispered, her fear making her think the worst.

"That's only in fairy tales," Ryan scoffed as only a big, grown-up five-year-old could. He stared at the man still standing off to one side, his dark figure partially obscured by the steadily thickening fog. "Are you magic?" he challenged.

The man chuckled. "Magic? No, I'm afraid not, son. My name is Jack, and I've recently moved here from a place far away. I can't leave you here this late at night, so what do you say to a ride?"

"We can trust him," Ryan said firmly.

"Ryan!" Caroline was shocked. "I'll tell Mom you talked to a stranger."

"We can't tell Mom anything, and you know it." He lowered his voice. "Besides, I think he's supposed to be here." With growing confidence, he walked toward Jack. "And I'm getting cold." The moisture from the fog had seeped through his thin T-shirt.

Caroline was also feeling the midnight chill, but the mysterious man's offer wasn't helping any. Still, she knew she couldn't abandon her brother the way Kevin had abandoned them.

Jack turned and gestured toward the road. He then walked away, aware of the two children slowly following him, pushing a rusty little bike.

He smiled as he thought of what he'd heard a few minutes before. So these two wanted a father badly enough to allow that other youngster to feed them a line about magic spells. He sensed three dollars was a lot for them to pay the little con artist in hopes of conjuring up a father. He glanced back at the children and noticed they'd left something behind. "Shouldn't you bring the book?" he asked.

Ryan looked over his shoulder and shook his head. "Let Kevin get in trouble for taking one of his mom's books. If Mom finds us out of bed, we're gonna be in enough trouble."

Jack smiled. "How old are you?"

"Five. Caroline, my sister, is seven. I'll be six real soon," he proudly announced.

Jack's smile dimmed. Five years old and already acting like the man of the house. Judging from the comments he heard earlier, the father had left the family for some woman named Eileen.

When they reached his parked car, he opened the passenger door for the kids and their bike and walked around to the driver's side.

Caroline hung back as she studied the low-slung black vehicle. "What if he flies away with us and we never see Mom again?" she murmured.

Ryan shot her a look. "Caro, he won't hurt us," he assured her, pulling on her hand. "Come on."

Nervously recalling every horror story of children being kidnapped and never heard from again she'd ever heard, Caro watched the streets whiz by as Ryan directed Jack to their house. What would happen to their mother if they were kidnapped? She didn't have any money to ransom them. Caro had overheard her tell Aunt Ivy their dad's support checks were never any good.

She stifled a sob, but Jack heard the muffled cry. "Here you are, Caroline, home safe and sound," he said quietly as he parked at the house Ryan indicated. He climbed out of the car and walked around to open the door for them. He hefted the bike to the sidewalk.

"We'll have to go in the way we came out," Ryan explained in a hushed voice, staring at the man he believed more and more was the result of Kevin's spell. "Thank you," he said belatedly.

Jack smiled. Children who believed in magic, and well mannered, too. "You're very welcome. All I ask is that you don't do this again," he cautioned. "Next time you might not be so lucky."

Caro nodded her head so hard it threatened to fall off. She edged away, wanting nothing more than to run into the house and hide under her bed. With luck, perhaps she'd wake up in the morning and realize this was all a bad dream.

Ryan remained steadfast. "You were worth the three dollars," he announced. "Don't take too long seeing Mom," he called softly over his shoulder before running off, Caro hot on his heels.

Jack stood by the car, watching the two children quietly park the bicycle near the front porch, then carefully open a window and crawl inside. He looked around the neighborhood, noting its shabby gentility. Despite their carefully tended yards and gardens, the houses had clearly seen better days. He glanced once more at the children's home, with its faded paint and unevenly cut lawn, then shook his head and drove off.

Two pair of eyes watched him from an upstairs window. "See? The fog is gone now," Ryan whispered to his sister. "And his car is black and very fast. He probably only drives it so people won't know he can fly. I told you he was magic."

"He can't be," Caro argued in a low voice as she jumped under her bedcovers. "Kevin was just playing a joke on us, and now we don't have the three dollars we saved up."

Ryan shook his head. "No, he's magic from Aunt Ivy's book, and he's gonna be our dad," he insisted. "You'll see. After all, everyone knows witchcraft works best here in Salem."

# *Chapter One*

"Celia always pays me in advance for the items I bring in." The silver-haired woman glared at Holly Bennett, who stood behind the glass-topped counter of Celia's Closet.

"Mrs. Benson, I cannot make any payments without Mrs. Parker's permission. We generally work on consignment, and since she hasn't marked any special instructions on your previous paperwork, my hands are tied," Holly explained, wishing she didn't sound so helpless. The other woman had the instincts of a shark. "Of course, you will receive payment at the beginning of the month for anything sold, and when Mrs. Parker comes back in a few days, you can speak to her about your usual arrangement."

Mrs. Benson started to pick up the items of clothing scattered across the counter, then abruptly moved away. "I'll leave them with you, but I want Celia to know about this the moment she returns. She'll make the necessary changes in my files so this doesn't happen again," she said haughtily, walking out of the store. The bell hanging above the door tinkled madly as the door swung shut.

Seconds later, a blonde swept in, her bright purple dress swirling around her calves.

"I see Winnie the witch was here." Ivy Elliott, a "professional divorcée," as she dubbed herself, and Holly's best friend, held up a steaming mug. "I figured you'd need some refreshment after the ordeal."

"You figured right." Holly gratefully accepted the black coffee. "No herb tea today?"

Ivy shook her head. "I was up till all hours yelling at Kevin. He was out doing God knows what until after midnight, and now *I'm* the one suffering from the lack of sleep while he's probably still in bed. Although, I told him if the lawn isn't mowed and the shrubs trimmed by the time I get home tonight, there's going to be hell to pay. I just know that kid will either end up in jail or in the marines when he turns eighteen. And I feel sorry for both institutions already." She leaned against the counter, waving an arm laden with multicolored bangle bracelets. "Then, to top it off, I've discovered that the antique volume of Elizabethan spells I found at that estate sale a month ago is missing. I had a buyer for it, too. Maybe my little angel found a way to make some money off it—by hocking it, no doubt."

Holly chuckled. "Come on, Ivy, Kevin's not all that bad. He's just having his identity crisis early in life." She scooped her bright auburn curls off her neck, pulled them up high and tied a wide band around her hair.

"It's disgusting that you have all that natural curl while my mop won't even hold a perm." Ivy wrinkled her nose. She wandered through the shop, picking up a blouse here, a scarf there. "You've got a lot of new things in."

Holly nodded. "Celia visited quite a few people before she left on vacation." She picked up a sheaf of inventory forms and said wryly, "Naturally, she was kind enough to leave me with the paperwork."

Ivy flipped through a jewelry carousel holding necklaces and bracelets. "I'm sure she deeply appreciates your efforts," she murmured sardonically.

"Don't start, Ivy."

The blonde was undeterred by her friend's slight censure. "Come on, Holly, we both know who really does all the work in this shop, and it isn't Celia Parker. Her idea of work is sipping tea with the moneyed classes and chatting them up while she looks over the wardrobes they replace each season. She takes their castoffs on consignment and acts as if she's doing them a wonderful service, while you're the one who coordinates outfits, displays them to their best advantage, and sells them as fast as they come in. Not to mention inventorying them, of course. You're the one who keeps this place going, not her."

"I only wish my castoff clothing looked so good," Holly said dryly, gesturing toward a designer dress displayed on the wall with appropriate accessories. "Besides, Celia lets me work around the kids' schedule, and you know how difficult it is to find an employer who will do that."

"Holly, I'm not trying to knock your job. I just wish—"

"Ivy," Holly interrupted, "when Ron left me, I had no job skills and no prospects. Celia was willing to take me on and train me. I know you don't like her, but she did take a chance in hiring me, and I'm grateful to her for that."

Ivy looked chastened. The Bennett divorce had provided the kind of juicy gossip any small town thrived on. But she, more than anyone, truly knew what Holly had been through since Ron Bennett decided he preferred the attentions of a local junior college prom queen to those of his wife and two young children.

"You're right," she ruefully admitted, placing a vibrant silk scarf on the counter. "Can you hold this for me and I'll pay for it when I close up next door?"

Holly picked up the scarf. "No problem."

Ivy glanced out the front window to see if anyone was lingering near her bookshop. Prospective customers for her stock of the latest thing in New Age occultism were valuable, and those looking for rare volumes dealing with ancient lore and authentic remedies from generations of wisewomen were even more valuable. "It's been slow all day, even with the tourists wandering around looking for signs of witches."

She lowered her voice and grinned. "Of course, perhaps they should come in here and meet the descendant of Priscilla Drake, the only witch in Salem to have been burned at the stake. You know, sweetie, if you'd lived back then, they probably would have taken one look at your 'witch's mark' and fiery hair and burned you, too."

Holly touched the small mole near her upper lip. "Maybe I would have been one of the lucky ones and only been hanged," she said wryly. "Isn't it amazing how this town's colorful seafaring history is completely overshadowed by our more violent past?"

"Yes, but it brings customers into my shop, so I can't complain," Ivy replied, brightening as she spotted two women entering her bookstore. "See you later." She scampered off, pausing to toss over her shoulder, "How much you want to bet one of those ladies hopes to find a spell that will help her lose twenty pounds overnight? Lord," she muttered, "if I had that kind of spell, I'd have given up dieting years ago!" With that, she was gone.

Holly turned to the pile of clothing Mrs. Benson had left. She figured she had a good hour's work ahead of her, listing each item by design, label, color, size, estimated retail price and the price Celia's Closet would sell it for. A copy of the list would be sent to Mrs. Benson and the original kept for the shop's use. Then she would have the task of making price tags and attaching them to each piece of clothing. She didn't mind the detailed work; it kept her mind off worries about finding the money for new storm windows for the house before the cold weather set in and wondering if the furnace would last another winter or choke to death in the middle of a snowstorm.

"It's only June, and you're already worrying about storm windows," she muttered, reaching for the inventory sheets. She was soon lost in her chore until the bell tinkling over the door alerted her to a prospective customer. She summoned up a smile. "Hello, Sally."

"Holly, my dear, how are you?" the slightly plump, dark-haired woman gushed as she swept through the shop, stopping every now and then to examine a dress or blouse. "My, you have some lovely things here. Of course, I would never dream of purchasing a piece of previously owned clothing. In my business, I have to project a successful image, and wearing last year's dress just wouldn't do."

Holly's smile froze. Temptation prompted her to ask why the gossipy Realtor was here, then past experience told her Sally Adams would get around to the reason for her visit sooner or later.

"Too bad, Sally. I received an outfit yesterday that would look stunning on you." She gestured toward a black-and-gold hip-length jacket over a black silk dress.

Sally examined the outfit, picked up the tag and uttered a throaty laugh not unlike a horse's neigh. "Holly, darling, this is much too large for me. You know very well I'm two sizes smaller."

Holly winced inwardly at the blatant fabrication, but she wasn't about to correct the tiresome woman.

"Holly, I know it must be difficult for you, having to raise those darling children of yours on your own while Ron shacks up with that bleached-blond beauty queen. And that huge house is such a drain on you financially. You three would be so much better off with a smaller place, and I just happen to have a listing for a nice little house on the outskirts of town."

"Thanks, Sally, but we're managing just fine where we are," Holly lied smoothly. The children had known enough chaos in their little lives; she'd be damned if she'd uproot them from their home just yet.

Sally looked annoyed, but then she brightened and brought out a bigger gun. "Holly, dear," she said dramatically, "I hate to carry tales when you already have so much on your plate. . . ."

"But?" Holly prompted, knowing the woman carried more tales than she did real-estate listings.

Sally looked suitably pained. "Well, I thought I saw your two little ones wandering in the vicinity of the Williams meadow late last night, and I was certain that hellion Kevin Elliott was with them. It's a shame Ivy can't keep a tighter rein on that boy. You just watch, he's going to come to a bad end some day."

Holly forced herself not to show her dismay. The children couldn't have been out last night. She'd put them to bed herself. She would have known if they'd left the house. Wouldn't she? Yet Ivy *had* complained that Kevin was out late last night....

"Thank you for caring, Sally." Her irony was lost on the woman. "But you must have been mistaken. Caroline and Ryan were both sound asleep late last night."

Sally looked dubious. "Well, dear, I'd hate to see anything happen to those two darling children of yours." She placed immaculately manicured blood-red nails against her plump chest. "Oh, by the way, you did hear that I sold the Williams house, didn't you?"

Holly was surprised she'd missed that piece of information. The four-story Victorian on the edge of town had a lurid history much discussed by Salem residents. "No, I'm afraid I hadn't. Congratulations."

Sally's eyes gleamed at her bit of one-upmanship, and, no doubt, at her commission on the sale. "Yes, a gentleman, recently moved here from Europe, wanted to purchase the house and meadow. He didn't quibble one bit on the price, and the financing went through without a hitch. A law firm in New York handled all the details and was very closemouthed about Mr. Montgomery's background. Can you imagine that he bought the house after only seeing pictures of it? I didn't even get to meet the man." She unintentionally showed her irritation at the lost opportunity for gossip about the mysterious newcomer to the community.

Holly hid a smile. "I guess he didn't mind the stories about the house's history."

"That it's haunted? That's what makes it so unique." Her eyes revealed a hint of worry that even sheer arrogance couldn't mask. "Besides," she said briskly, "we all know the rumors are nonsense. Nothing's ever been proved," she added a little too forcefully, highlighting her unease.

Holly wondered how much, if any, of the house's history the mysterious Mr. Montgomery had been allowed to hear. After all, how many people would willingly pay a huge price to live in a house rumored to be haunted by the original owner, who'd killed himself in it? "Well," the Realtor twittered, "I must be off. Take care, dear."

Holly chuckled and shook her head. Then her thoughts turned to the reason for Sally's visit, and all humor disappeared. Her conversation with her children that evening would be about a great deal more than their activities at day camp.

"WHEN YOU TOLD ME you bought a house, you didn't say it was a mausoleum."

Jack turned from watching the moving men place boxes in the high-ceilinged drawing room. The woman striding toward him was exquisite, from her tousled mane of honey-blond curls to her dainty feet shod in

Italian leather pumps. Her amber silk jumpsuit hugged every feminine curve, and her midnight-blue eyes sparkled.

"Darling, this house is ugly," she pronounced.

"You've hardly seen it," he protested.

"I don't have to. I'm sure its belfry houses bats, I see no evidence of central heating, and I wouldn't be surprised to hear the place is haunted." She tipped her head to one side, giving him a smile known to drive men to their knees.

This man remained standing. Having known the woman since her birth, he was immune to her abundant feminine charms. "You've just listed some of the reasons I bought it, Letitia." He draped an arm around her shoulders. "Come on, let me give you a tour."

Letitia's hand caressed the banister as they climbed the stairway to the second floor. "Jack, you're my brother, and I love you dearly, but this house is all wrong."

"Letitia, you're my sister, and I love you dearly," he softly mocked, "and it's perfect. I promise to give you full rein in decorating."

Letitia peeped into the rooms they passed. "I can do wonders come Halloween," she groused. "I can see it all now—cobwebs in the corners, fog seeping through the window sashes, candlelight only, since the antique wiring in this place will have blown by then. Perhaps a few choice bats flying through the belfry, maybe a body or two hanging in the closets." She spun on her heel, walking backward as they continued down the hallway, her hands moving gracefully with each word she spoke. "Jack, couldn't you work just as easily in

New York or Boston, or even in Los Angeles? Surely all that smog and crime would set your brain humming with ideas. Why here?"

"Because it has the atmosphere I want," he murmured, looking off into space. "The moment I saw the pictures of this house, I knew I could work here. When I walked in the front door, I was certain of it. If I'm to bring my work to the United States, I want to do it right. And this is the place to do it."

"Don't you think a horror specialist in Salem, Massachusetts, is just a bit much?"

He smiled. "Not at all. It's perfect."

Letitia threw up her hands. "All right, I know when I'm beaten. I'll create a home that will never be forgotten, but—" she pointed her forefinger at him in warning "—if one ghost appears in my bedroom in the dead of night, I will not be happy."

"And if the ghost is young, male and good-looking?" he teased.

"Then I'll reconsider, of course. Now show me the rest of the house before I change my mind. You can also tell me about your time here so far. Have you met anyone interesting?"

Jack immediately thought of the two children in the fog-shrouded meadow. The girl with her large green eyes and soulful expression, and the boy who barely looked school age and already took his family responsibilities seriously. He remembered them braving the midnight hour in the hopes that a spell cast by a young scam artist would bring them a father. And a puppy, he recalled with a smile. He wondered what kind of woman inspired two children to resort to magic to conjure up a husband for her.

"Aha, you've met a woman," Letitia gleefully pounced on her brother's expression.

"No, not a woman. Just . . . a bit of witchcraft," he murmured. "But that's what Salem is known for. Witchcraft."

"HOLLY, YOU CAN'T believe Sally Adams's every malicious tale," Ivy told her as they walked down the tree-lined street to their respective homes. "She likes nothing more than to stir up trouble, and what better way than to have you worry about Ryan and Caro traipsing around late at night? Besides, can you honestly believe they'd go to the Williams meadow after dark, with all the stories about its being haunted? Kevin, maybe, but not them."

Holly gazed morosely ahead. "She sounded so sure of herself, even as she put in her little dig about Ron."

"She's just jealous because you got Ron even though she had the hots for him."

"Yes, but I wasn't able to keep him."

Ivy grabbed her friend's shoulders, forcing her to stop in her tracks. "If Ron came crawling to your door tonight, begging you to take him back, would you?"

She didn't need to think about her reply. "Of course not! Although I sincerely doubt he'd come crawling back when he's having so much fun with Eileen Butkus."

Ivy scowled. "How I'd love to put a hex on that man so all his so-called important body parts would fall off. That would sure ruin his fun."

Holly started laughing so hard she almost choked. "Oh, Ivy, what would I do without you?"

"You're never going to find out. Now, just consider Sally's story nothing more than *her* brand of mischief. And give her time. Pretty soon she'll be off making someone else's life miserable."

"Did you hear about her selling the Williams house and property?" Holly asked as they continued walking.

Ivy was stunned. "Really? So she managed to find a sucker for that monstrosity, did she? I bet old Humphrey must be excited to have someone to haunt again."

Holly defended the old house. "I don't think it's a monstrosity. It's just been sitting empty all these years and needs some love and attention, that's all."

"I know how much you love that relic, but it needs more than that. Old Humphrey Williams has haunted that house since the eighteen-hundreds when he killed himself. It should be torn down so he can go off to wherever displaced ghosts go."

Holly stopped at the walk leading to her house, raising her eyebrows at the ear-splitting music coming from the house next door. The house Ivy shared with her eleven-year-old son, who thought the height of fashion was dressing like G.I. Joe.

Ivy winced. "Forget Sally's story. Your two at their worst is a piece of cake compared to my one at his best. Too bad he had to take after his father." She grimaced and headed up her front walk. "See ya tomorrow."

Holly glanced at her own front porch. It seemed to sag more each day. As part of the divorce settlement, her ex-husband was supposed to make necessary repairs on the house, but he always seemed to have a logical excuse ready any time she approached him on the subject. And she couldn't afford a handyman, or someone to paint the exterior, which sorely needed sprucing up.

When she entered the house, the aroma from the casserole she'd defrosted that morning was wafting through the downstairs, and her children were seated at the dining room table. Caroline read aloud to Ryan, who listened as he busily crayoned in his coloring book. She was pleased at the happy family image but sad that she hadn't gotten home earlier to be there to greet *them*. With Celia away, she'd run later than usual. Well, she'd simply have to try harder. Five and seven was way too young for them to become latch-key kids.

Hearing her approach, both children looked up with broad smiles.

"I was milk monitor today at snack time," Ryan proudly announced, jumping up and running over to throw his arms around Holly's legs.

Caroline rolled her eyes. "Big deal. They choose the milk monitor alphabetically."

Holly sent her daughter a mildly censuring look. "It's a very big deal to do it well." She dropped a kiss on her son's head.

"I put the casserole in the oven so it would be ready in about twenty minutes," Caroline said, marking her place and closing the book. "And it's Ryan's turn to set the table."

"First I'm a milk monitor, now I'm a maid," he grumbled, trudging off to the kitchen.

Holly chuckled. "Poor baby." She draped an arm around Caroline's shoulders. "How was your day?"

She shrugged. "It was okay."

Holly watched her daughter with concern. Even at five Ryan acted more assured than many children several years his senior, but Caroline was as shy as her mother. While she had friends and did well in school, she seemed to keep too much inside. Holly tried to draw her out, but her ex-husband had often neglected his daughter while loudly planning things he and his son would do together when Ryan was older. Somehow Holly doubted Ron would change when Ryan reached whatever that all-important age was that would make him a suitable companion.

Truth be told, the more she thought about it, the less she could imagine Caro out in the Williams meadow late last night. The girl couldn't even stand to listen to the tamest of ghost stories. Ivy was right. Sally's story was simply mischief or a case of mistaken identity.

"What did you do in day camp today?"

Caroline shrugged again. "Mrs. Chandler started us on making a papier-mâché recreation of Old Salem for Parents Day."

Holly smiled. "I can't wait to see it."

Caroline chewed on her lower lip. "Mom, do you believe in magic?"

"Magic? Like the magician we saw on TV last week?"

She shook her head. "No, like the magic witches do. Spells to make things happen or make people from magazines real."

Holly drew her closer to her side. "Honey, you know all that is nothing more than fairy tales. There's really no such thing as witches or witchcraft," she said gently.

Caroline looked up, her tiny face so serious it almost broke Holly's heart. What was bothering her so much? "What about the books Aunt Ivy sells? Don't they make things happen?"

"Caro, sweetie, what are you getting at?"

Ryan entered the room and glared at his sister. "Hey, move, I gotta put these plates down," he said, elbowing her aside.

"Oh, I was just curious," Caroline muttered to her mother, looking away.

"All right." Holly combed her fingers through Caroline's ponytail, which had started its usual end-of-the-day drooping. "I'd better get the vegetables on. You two wash up for dinner, okay?"

"Good going," Ryan muttered as they headed for the bathroom. "You almost gave it away."

"What we did was wrong," she retorted. "And what if Kevin's spell gives us a dad we don't like? What do we do then?"

Ryan was undeterred. "Then we'll send him back and do it again." He ran ahead into the bathroom.

Caroline sighed. "I don't think Kevin will do it for free, and we don't have any more money."

"If he screws it up he'll do it for free or I'll punch him one," he threw over his shoulder.

"He's bigger than you."

"So what? He promised it would work, and it will. I want a dad, and I want a puppy." Ryan slammed the door behind him.

Caroline leaned against the closed door. "I wish I'd been an only child."

"DID YA MEET ANYONE new today, Mom?" Ryan asked brightly, digging into the casserole.

Holly looked up. "I meet new people almost every day," she said. "Was I supposed to meet someone in particular today?"

He shook his head quickly. "No, I was just wondering, that's all."

"Mrs. Benson came in."

Ryan groaned. "She smells funny, and she always pats me on the head like a dog and calls me her little man."

"She acts like she thinks she's a queen or something," Caroline piped up.

Holly hid her smile. Their description of Winifred Benson was right on the mark. The woman always wore a heavy perfume and prided herself on tracing her family back to the original settlement of Salem. That Holly's own roots could be traced back just as far didn't count, since Holly had clearly married beneath herself, as even Holly's own parents had lamented until their deaths. Not to mention that Holly had, saints preserve us, a witch on her family tree.

"Just be grateful she doesn't expect us to curtsy when she enters a room."

SOON AFTER DINNER, Holly tucked her two sleepy children into their beds. With the rest of the evening in front of her, she opted for her favorite form of relaxation: a bubble bath.

A few minutes later, with a paperback novel in hand, and with soothing music from the cassette player in her bedroom drifting into the steamy bathroom, she stepped into the hot, lightly scented water and settled back with a sigh. As she gazed at the couple in a rhapsodic embrace on the cover of her novel, then down at the lush bubbles dotting her pale skin, she admitted she was an incurable romantic, even if the one time she fell in love turned out to be the worst mistake she ever made.

Her ears took in the sweet classical music, and she smiled. "All I need now is a man to make bath time more interesting," she said out loud. Then she laughed softly at her own nonsense. She was too busy to let herself miss that all-important part of her life. Most of the time. Besides, she'd had a man in her life once, and look what happened. Still, she had two wonderful children.

A LOW-SLUNG BLACK CAR too elegant for the neighborhood cruised slowly down the street where Holly Bennett lived, slowing to a crawl in front of her house. The driver looked up at the lit window misted with steam. When the car window slid noiselessly down, the faint strains of a Strauss waltz were audible from an open upstairs window.

The driver smiled. He'd already glimpsed Caroline and Ryan's mother on her walk home earlier tonight. Coppery red curls that defied a brush, a too-slender body and a face that was more cute than beautiful. Not the type of woman he'd been with in the past—the ones who wore designer originals, drank vintage champagne and danced till dawn under disco lights, pausing only for affairs with no strings attached. So why did this sprite with two very tangible strings attached fascinate him so much? The window slid upward, sealing the air-conditioned interior of the car.

"Perhaps they performed witchcraft, after all," he said to himself as he stepped on the accelerator and left the neighborhood.

# Chapter Two

"Where can they be?" Holly searched the magazine rack, then checked under the newspaper spread on the coffee table. She uttered a cry of irritation when she found what she was looking for. "Caroline! Ryan!"

The two children ran into the room, skidding to a stop in front of their frustrated-looking mother. "What have you done?" She held up the mutilated magazines.

They shifted uneasily.

"You mean to the *Newsweek* and *Redbook*?" Caro asked haltingly.

Holly nodded. "That's exactly what I mean. Why didn't you ask me before you made cutouts? Not only haven't I read them yet, but they're Aunt Ivy's, and I planned to give them back to her when I finished."

"Back to her?" Caro echoed numbly.

"It was a camp project," Ryan piped up, a little too quick with his answer.

She looked at her son suspiciously. "And you couldn't ask first?"

He looked shamefaced. "I forgot. Sorry, Mom."

Holly turned to her daughter. "What about you, Caro? You know better."

Caro stared down at her feet. "I'm sorry."

If there was more to the story, neither one was giving anything away. Holly sighed. For the past week or so, the children had been awfully mysterious about something. "You will apologize to Aunt Ivy for what you've done, and next time, make sure you ask permission." After receiving nods from both, she indicated they were free to leave the room. "Something is very wrong here," she murmured, tossing the torn magazines into the wastebasket. "I only hope I can survive the next fifteen years."

"ALL OF A SUDDEN they keep secrets," Holly told Ivy as they shared a quick lunch in the back of Ivy's store. "You know Caroline. She'd die before she'd tell a lie. Yet I could swear she was hiding something from me. It's downright scary, Ivy."

"You want scary, I'll lend you Kevin for a few days." She speared a piece of lettuce from her take-out container. "I've even considered torture to get him to admit he took that volume of Elizabethan spells. I told him I have a buyer for it, and that if it doesn't show up within the next forty-eight hours, he'll be grounded for the next fifty years. All he does is spout name, rank and serial number and insist he doesn't know anything about it."

Holly shook her head in wonderment. "What would Kevin do with a book of spells? Did it have any pertaining to turning someone into the ultimate warrior?"

Ivy shook her head. "Nope. This book dealt purely with love. Aphrodisiac spells, fertility rites—that kind of thing. You know, where you take a likeness of your true love and sprinkle it with a special potion while standing in a crossroads at midnight on the summer solstice."

Holly was fascinated. "A likeness? Like a painting?"

She nodded. "Back then, yes. A painting, or a silhouette, or a drawing, perhaps. These days I suppose it would be a photo. You know, if I thought it would work, I'd clip some pictures of Harrison Ford and Mel Gibson and stand in the middle of the town square chanting my lungs out. Then I'd lock myself away with the two of them for the next twenty years."

"Too bad the summer solstice has just passed," she teased.

"I'd be willing to wait a year. Of course, in the meantime, I'd lose ten pounds and have a face-lift and a tummy tuck." Ivy tossed her lunch container into the trash and eyed the coconut macaroons she'd bought. "A nice, healthy salad for lunch, then these. I'm such a hypocrite," she said, sighing as she bit into a cookie with obvious relish.

Holly chuckled. "Ryan would use a spell like that to get himself a puppy—conveniently forgetting to conjure up dog food, of course."

"Speaking of food, if you're my friend, you'll help me eat these macaroons before I make a pig of myself," Ivy announced. "You can afford the extra calories."

Holly took a cookie.

"Want to hear the latest about the new owner of the old Williams place?" Ivy asked slyly.

Holly looked up. "It depends on where you heard it."

"Fact, not rumor. Sally was down at The Black Cauldron last night crowing about what she considers her ultimate deal. Of course, she's ticked off that a New York law firm acted on behalf of the buyer, so she wasn't able to meet him personally, but she did say the name of the buyer is Pyewacket International." Her eyes danced with laughter.

Holly frowned. The name sounded familiar, but the origin eluded her. "Pyewacket?"

"The cat from *Bell, Book and Candle.* The *witch's* cat," she continued. "Aunt Prudence said it's really Stephen King using another cover, since everyone already knows his Richard Bachman pseudonym. And Aunt Patience said it's really old Humphrey Williams come back to life. If it was old Humphrey, how unfortunate for him that he'd have to buy his own house."

Holly loved Ivy's wacky great-aunts. The Tutweiler sisters were well-known in Salem as psychics who hadn't gotten one prediction right in their eighty-some years of life. No one minded, though. The sweet old ladies were the very picture of gentler days gone by.

"Now I'm trying to find out the owner's birth date so I can draw up his chart," Ivy said, snagging another macaroon.

"Why?"

"To see if his star signs align favorably with yours, of course."

Though Ivy was a single mom, too, she was always far more ready to matchmake for Holly than she was to take the plunge herself. ''No, thanks, I have enough problems.'' Holly stood. ''Now that Celia's back, I'd better get back before she thinks I've dropped off the face of the earth.''

''Celia should kiss the earth you walk on,'' Ivy predictably retorted. ''I have no idea how you put up with her.''

Holly tugged her ginger-colored cotton sweater over the waistband of her floral skirt, straightening the strands of antique copper-and-brass beads that completed the look. ''It's the only way I can afford clothes, since Ryan seems to need a new pair of shoes every two weeks, and Caro refuses to stop growing,'' she quipped, walking to the door. ''See you later.''

When Holly stepped into Celia's Closet, she could hear her boss on the telephone using the low, soothing sounds that indicated she was talking to an important ''client.''

''Yes, Mrs. Nelson, I can make the time to come out to see you next week,'' Celia Parker cooed into the receiver. Her cool blue eyes glanced at Holly, then at the clock. Since Holly technically had two more minutes on her lunch hour, the older woman couldn't say anything. Celia enjoyed little more than finding fault with people. ''Wednesday at two. See you then. Goodbye, dear.'' She hung up and penned the date in her leather-bound appointment book. ''Too bad. Most of her clothing is too trendy for us, anyway.'' She lit a cigarette and drew the smoke deeply into her lungs. Celia firmly believed smoking could cause cancer—but not in her. In her mind, she was immune to everything, including good manners toward her employees. "I thought the front window display was to be changed yesterday," she said pointedly.

"It was very busy in here yesterday, and it's difficult to work in the window and wait on customers at the same time."

"Yes, I saw the receipts. Not bad," Celia said blandly.

Holly bit her lip to keep from blurting that the sales from the day before were the best in six months. It wouldn't do any good. Celia had only one passion—Celia.

"Why don't you change the display now. I'm still here in case someone comes in." The order sounded only remotely like a suggestion.

Holly held back a sigh of resignation. In reality, if anyone came in, Celia would merely call her from the window to handle the sale. Selling was clearly beneath Celia Parker. She enjoyed the idea of owning a shop, and it entitled her to enter the homes of the incredibly rich.

"Fine." She headed for the rear of the shop to put her purse away.

"Excuse me, ladies?"

Both women looked up at the sound of a man's voice. Celia was the first to react with a lift of her delicately arched brows and an almost feral smile on her red-glossed lips. She patted her pale blond chignon and rose to her feet, smoothing her silk dress over her hips. Holly stood off to one side, wondering how they had missed hearing the bells that hung over the door announce the man's entrance.

"Yes, may I help you?" Celia practically purred.

The man stood just inside the door. The afternoon sun flowing through the windows highlighted coal-black hair brushing the collar of a black polo shirt tucked neatly into black slacks. His body was lean, like a runner's. With his lofty height, deep tan and even deeper brown eyes, he looked like a dark angel, Holly thought. Something about him was very unsettling.

"I understand you take clothing on consignment," he said, his dark eyes resting on Holly.

"Yes, we do," Celia said. "I'm Celia Parker, the owner." She offered an immaculately manicured hand that boasted long, cherry-red nails. "I gather your wife is wishing to discard last season's wardrobe? Or perhaps you're disposing of an ex-wife's closet?" she asked coyly.

"Actually, I have some period clothing that appears to be in excellent condition." His hand barely brushed Celia's. "My name is Jack Montgomery. I recently moved into an old house at the edge of town, and I discovered several trunks of antique clothing in the attic. After making some inquiries, I was told your shop handled such things for costume rentals."

Celia's ice-blue eyes lit up at the prospect of profits. "I'm honored you came to me. What house did you purchase, Mr. Montgomery?"

Holly already knew the answer.

The man's eyes skimmed over her as he replied, "The Williams house, they call it. Perhaps your assistant could come out and take a look at what I have," he suggested, still looking at Holly rather than at Celia.

The older woman's face tightened, but she managed to maintain a smile. "Holly works in the shop. I handle the in-home consultations." She reached for her appointment book and leafed through the pages. "I could see you tomorrow at ten."

"I was told that Mrs. Bennett is the expert on period clothing, while you, Miss Parker, are the undisputed master—or should I say mistress—of today's fashions," he said graciously, smoothly undercutting Celia's manipulations. "I'm sure my sister would more than appreciate your assistance when she's ready to, shall we say, recycle the wardrobe she brought from Europe, but I hope you understand why I'd like Mrs. Bennett to look over the clothing in the attic."

Celia stared up at him. "Certainly," she said in a taut voice, not bothering to consult Holly. "Holly can be there tomorrow morning."

Holly's eyes widened. "But—"

"I can certainly look after the store for a few hours," Celia said firmly, shooting her employee a look. "I'm sure you'll be able to give Mr. Montgomery whatever assistance he requires."

The man's midnight eyes seemed to engulf Holly in a swirling moonlit fog, and she felt a tingling sensation skitter across her nerve endings. What was happening here?

"Ten—ten o'clock?" she stammered.

He smiled. "Actually, eleven would be better. I do a great deal of my work at night and generally sleep late."

"Eleven o'clock," she agreed softly.

He smiled again, a polite, dangerous, masculine smile, not looking the least abashed at being surrounded by feminine fashions. "Shall I write out directions to my home, Mrs. Bennett?"

Holly shook her head. "We're all familiar with the Williams— I guess we should call it the Montgomery house now."

"Whatever pleases you." With a nod, he walked out of the store as silently as he had entered.

"Those bells are useless," Celia sputtered, clearly furious at being outmaneuvered. "They don't even work half the time."

Holly wondered. They had rung incessantly the day before as people had wandered in and out of the shop.

"When you look over the clothing, downplay it as much as possible," Celia crisply instructed. "Check for loose seams, moth holes, torn or discolored lace— anything to keep the price down. If the items are as good as he claims, I intend to make a large profit from rentals, and I *don't* intend to cut him in on it."

"I'm surprised he doesn't want to donate any of it to the historical society," Holly mused.

Celia snorted. "Obviously, the man doesn't need a tax write-off. Take the Polaroid camera to photograph the best pieces, and make detailed notes on the rest. I'll take it from there. Also—" she glanced with distaste over Holly's outfit "—make sure you dress professionally tomorrow. If necessary, borrow something from the shop. After all, you are representing me. We can't have you looking like a mere housewife, can we?"

Holly nodded, ignoring Celia's customary rudeness. Her boss's words weren't truly registering, anyway. She was still thinking about the man who sent those shivers up and down her spine. How on earth was she going to handle tomorrow?

"SO WHO WAS THE HUNK in your shop today?" Ivy asked eagerly as she and Holly began their walk home that evening. "And can he string two words together? Not that it matters, with a body like that! Those all-brawn, no-brains types can be perfect for a quick fling."

Holly smiled mysteriously. "He just moved to town, and he found some period clothing in the attic of the mansion he bought. He wants to sell the stuff to Celia."

Ivy's eyes lit up. "Are you saying *he's* the one who bought old Humphrey Williams's house?"

Holly nodded smugly upon delivering the tantalizing bit of gossip.

But Ivy's face fell. "Oh, no," she muttered to herself. "His aura . . ."

"What was wrong with his aura? Was it plaid? Did it have purple polka dots all over it?" Holly teased.

Ivy frowned. She took the subject very seriously. "No, that I could almost handle," she murmured. "What was so strange was that I couldn't detect any aura at all."

Holly didn't tease her further. Ivy prided herself on her ability to read people's auras, and Holly had to admit her friend was correct ninety percent of the time.

"His name is Jack Montgomery," she offered. "And he said something about a sister. I gather she lives with him."

"No wife?"

"Celia practically came right out and asked him, but he never really answered her," she replied thoughtfully.

"He was probably put off by those bug-spray fumes Celia calls a custom-blended perfume."

Holly's nervousness about her upcoming appointment with the mysterious Jack Montgomery was returning. "I'm going out there tomorrow to look over the clothing."

Ivy's brows lifted in shock. "And Celia's letting you?" Then she answered her own question. "All those books on period clothing you always pore over.... I guess even she has to admit you know more about the subject than she does."

"Mr. Montgomery made the suggestion. I think his oblique offer of allowing Celia the first look at his sister's European wardrobe clinched it."

Ivy muttered a few uncomplimentary words about the woman under her breath. "Then do us both a favor and find out his birth time and date. Although, after not seeing an aura, I don't think he's meant for you, sweetie," she said apologetically. "I need to find someone with a very warm aura for you."

"Ivy, I have enough going on right now without a man messing up my life even more."

Ivy patted her friend's arm. "You've got to get over this shyness of yours, Holly. It's crippling your social life."

"I can't hold my family together and have a social life at the same time. Besides, most men don't jump at the chance to date a woman with two small children in tow."

"The right one will," Ivy said with confidence. "Too bad that book of spells is missing. Otherwise I'd try one on you."

Holly moaned. Ivy had been her closest friend for years, but once the woman got her teeth into a project, she didn't let go.

It was probably a good thing Jack Montgomery didn't have an aura visible to Ivy's sharp eye. The man was already disturbing enough. It was as if some powerful force within him disrupted the demeanor of anyone in his path. He'd certainly mesmerized the unflappable Celia, and now he had Ivy climbing walls. Holly couldn't help but wonder what would happen to her after a few hours in his company. But then, she reminded herself, she would only be looking over some clothing, probably alone. A man who wore raw-silk slacks and handmade leather loafers wouldn't knock about in a musty old attic.

"WITCHES, WITCHES, everywhere," Letitia chanted, entering Jack's office with her usual exuberant theatrics.

He didn't look up from his computer screen. "Out."

"Jack, my love, let's go into Boston for dinner. Someplace where I can speak French or Italian to the maître d'. Where the waiters are snobbier than the diners."

"You're the snob, Ticia."

"True," she said easily. She dropped into an easy chair. "Jack, that housekeeper you hired looks as if she's lived here since the witch trials. In fact, she's probably the head crone in these parts."

He didn't look away from his work. "Mrs. Boggs comes highly recommended. Now get out so I can finish these notes."

Letitia combed her fingers through her long mane of honey-blond hair. "I'm certain this house has mice along with the ghosts."

"Then that snobbish excuse for a cat you have should have a good time catching them, shouldn't he? After all, that's what cats are good for."

She gasped in horror. "Le Chat abhors mice! Just seeing one would upset him. He's very sensitive, Jack."

Jack turned his head. "Ticia, you're annoying me," he said, amusement and brotherly love undercutting the firmness of his message.

She pouted and gracefully flopped back in the chair. "Jack, this house is giving me nightmares."

"Then, beloved brat, drive into Boston on your own," he suggested. "I have work to do. Or, if it's that bad, fly to London for a few days to visit Mom, or go on to Paris."

"Oh, no, I intend to see this to the bitter end." Her rolling eyes indicated the sacrifice she was making on his behalf.

His grin lightened his dark features. "Your sisterly devotion is touching."

Brother and sister might argue or tease, but they were always there for each other, no matter what. And Jack wondered what Letitia would think of Holly Bennett when she met her the next day.

"WE STILL WANT our money back!" Uncaring that his opponent obviously outweighed him, Ryan advanced on Kevin.

"Why should I give you your money back when the spell worked?" he argued.

"Did not!"

"It sure did! I saw that guy, remember? And I heard my mom tell Great-Aunt Prudence your mom is going out to his house tomorrow. So they'll see each other and fall in love and get married, just like you want them to." Kevin smirked.

Caroline wasn't convinced. "But he's made from magic! How can Mom fall in love with a man who isn't real?"

Kevin shrugged. "You asked for a dad. I got you one. You didn't say what kind. Besides, he looks just like one of the pictures you gave me. I did better than I figured I would." He beamed with pride. "In fact, if I can do that good, I just might advertise around school. I could make a lot of money."

"Caro said the dad plan won't work because the guy isn't real," Ryan argued, narrowing his eyes until they were mere slits. He raised one clenched fist. "Give us back our money, Kevin Elliott, or I'll bust you in the nose!"

"Ryan!"

His shoulders dropped at the sound of his mother's horrified voice. He was well and truly caught.

Holly ran into the yard and grasped her son's shoulders. "I can't believe you were threatening Kevin," she scolded.

"It was his fault," he muttered, feeling his mother's hands push him back toward the house. Now he was probably going to lose TV for a week, all because of creepy Kevin!

"I don't care who started it, you don't fight." Holly turned back to Kevin. "And, Kevin, I'm ashamed of you for leading on a little boy."

"Little?" he scoffed. "Ryan can beat up kids bigger'n me!"

Holly's shocked gasp told him that wasn't what she wanted to hear.

"I won't tease him anymore, Holly," he assured her. While Kevin might be a con artist in the making, he truly adored Holly Bennett, with her sweet smile and her gentle ways. His mom once said Holly was too sweet and shy for her own good, and since then he had gone out of his way not to upset her. Upsetting his own mother was another story, of course. She could handle the stress of dealing with a kid like him.

"Kevin Elliott, you're a real creep for getting Ryan into trouble," Caroline hotly accused him the moment her mother was out of earshot.

"What do you want me to do? Prove the guy is real?"

He wondered, though. After all, there had been that strange fog in the meadow that night, and the man had just appeared out of nowhere. And what normal guy would buy a haunted house? Wouldn't it be something if he wasn't real? Then again, what if he turned out to be a ghoul and did something terrible to Holly?

Maybe he really should find out, Kevin decided.

Who knows? Kevin Elliott might even turn out to be a hero for rescuing Holly from some blood-sucking vampire!

His narrow chest puffed out. "Don't you worry, Caro. I'll make sure everything is okay," he assured the girl. "If the guy is made of magic, I'll send him back where he belongs."

Caroline still didn't look convinced. "With our luck you'll only make things worse. Besides, once your mom discovers it was you who took her book of spells, you're going to be in so much trouble you'll be grounded for good.''

''Mom has more to worry about than me.''

''That's not what she says.''

## *Chapter Three*

"Mom, I've told you a million times I didn't take that stupid book. Why don't you believe me?" Kevin sat at the kitchen table looking as innocent as a newborn babe.

"Probably because your checkered past won't allow me to believe you." Ivy poured her third cup of coffee. "Not to mention you've been showing an unusual interest in my books lately."

"Maybe I'm taking after you," he said piously.

Ivy rolled her eyes. "Pull the other leg, sweetheart. I know you too well. Look, Kevin, I have an interested buyer who will pay a pretty penny for that volume. If you bring it back in good condition, I won't punish you for taking it. Otherwise, you might not see the light of day for the next hundred years."

Kevin thought of the book lying in the middle of the meadow. By now it was probably ruined, he figured. And his mother wouldn't hesitate to ground him for the rest of his life. He was better off sticking to the story that he didn't take it. Maybe he could go out to the meadow today, find the book, sneak it back into the house and hide it in the cellar or something.

"Kevin, are you even listening to me?" His mother's question brought him back to the present.

He looked up guiltily. "I was thinking about going through all your books for you, even in the attic and cellar," he suggested. "Maybe it got mixed up with some of the others."

Ivy looked skeptical. "I doubt it, but a good cleaning in the attic and cellar wouldn't hurt. You can start today."

Kevin groaned. "Mom!" Having neatly consigned him to a week of slavery, his mother smugly set down her coffee cup and headed for the front door to retrieve the morning paper.

"Jeez, she's really going to make me suffer for this," Kevin said, sighing, pouring more maple syrup on his cornflakes, a concoction that made his mother shudder.

"Kevin! Come here!"

He dropped his head to the tabletop. "What'd I do now?" he groaned.

"Kevin!"

"Yeah, I'm coming." He slowly pushed back his chair and stood up, weighing the odds of making a successful escape out the back door.

Too late.

"Look at this! I found it on the doormat." His mother thrust a paper-wrapped package under his nose, its strings loosened to reveal the volume of Elizabethan spells Kevin had used in the meadow. "It's my book!" she squealed. "I don't know how, I don't know why, but it's back. Kevin, sweetheart, I owe you an apology." She hugged him tightly. "Now I know you didn't take it, because you could never wrap a package worth a damn. I'm just so glad it's back!"

Kevin stared at the book. It looked the same as it had three nights ago, and no worse for wear. He had no idea how it had gotten to their front porch—unless it had sprouted legs and walked. The longer he looked at its faded gilt lettering and black cloth cover, the heavier his breakfast settled in his stomach.

"Isn't it amazing? Here I was talking about it, and it suddenly showed up," Ivy babbled.

"Yeah, amazing," he said. Apparently if a book of witchcraft wanted to return home badly enough, it could do it in the most obvious way. Via witchcraft.

"MOM, DAD'S HERE."

Caroline's flat announcement was another proverbial nail in Holly's coffin. She'd been up half the night with Ryan, who'd suffered an upset stomach after too much cake, ice cream and pizza at a friend's birthday party the evening before. After crawling back into bed at 4:00 a.m., it was inevitable she would sleep through her alarm and have to rush around getting the kids ready for day camp while simultaneously gearing herself up for her visit to the Williams—correction, Montgomery—house. The dress she'd planned to wear had a stain squarely in the front, Caroline was in tears because she couldn't find her favorite blouse, and Ryan loudly complained that after being sick last night he shouldn't be forced to go to day camp. And now Holly had her ex-husband to contend with.

"Oh, joy," she muttered between clenched teeth as she headed downstairs. "Hello, Ron."

Ron Bennett, once Salem's heartthrob and now the high school's baseball coach, flashed that old smile that used to turn Holly's bones to jelly.

"Just thought I'd come by to see the kids," he greeted her. "You know, you really should have some work done around here, Holly. The place is starting to looking pretty shabby."

She mentally counted to ten. "According to the courts, house repairs are up to you. Caro and Ryan leave for day camp in five minutes. You should have called first."

He spread his hands out in front of him. "Hey, babe, I've got a full schedule. Look, have someone come in and do the work, and I'll reimburse you."

Holly knew that line only too well. In the two years they'd been divorced Ron hadn't paid out one penny more than he absolutely had to, and even then he took his own sweet time doing it. He was constantly several months behind in child support, and the few times he grudgingly did pay on time, his checks usually bounced. This wasn't the first time Holly wished she had a more forceful personality, so she could stand up to Ron better.

"I hope you're planning to make that last check of yours good," she said.

Ron stared at her as if she'd said something obscene. "You know, Holly, it's that bitching of yours that drove me away in the first place."

She opened her mouth to argue—nagging was the last thing she'd ever done, since he was barely ever home long enough for her to complain about anything—then she closed it again. "The day camp fees are due the first of the month," was all she said. She wished that just once she'd have the nerve to say what she really felt: that Ron was the lowest of lows at parenting, and that he didn't deserve the two wonderful children he had fathered. "You agreed to cover the camp costs."

His expression tightened, but he pulled a checkbook out of his back pocket, quickly scrawled out a check and threw it to her. "I don't know why I should pay all my life for kids I never wanted in the first place." He spun on his heel and stalked off.

It wasn't until his car roared off that Holly released the breath she'd been holding. She bent down slowly and picked up the check.

"Holly, my sweet, you look like a thundercloud." Ivy crossed the yard. "I suppose we have your charming ex to thank for that?"

"I'm a wimp," Holly muttered sadly. "I've never been able to confront the man. Even Ryan does a better job of standing up to people than I do. I'm just glad he and Caro weren't around to hear his obnoxious comments."

"Oh, you've got the guts," Ivy said. "You simply haven't found them yet. The day that happens, I want to be around, because Ron will be in for the surprise of his life!" She noticed Holly's black skirt and ivory, lace-trimmed blouse. "Aren't we a bit conservative for Celia's Closet?"

"I'm going out to Mr. Montgomery's house this morning, and Celia wants me to look professional."

Ivy nodded. "Oh, yes, the hunk without an aura. So why are you dressed for a funeral? The man *is* good-looking, Holly, even if he isn't your Mr. Right. You can still use him for practice until the right man comes along."

Holly thought of the dark eyes that had watched her so intently the day before and repressed a shiver. "Practice? Not on this one."

"Look, just because I missed his aura doesn't necessarily mean he's totally unsuitable. I'll need to study him more, that's all. He's certainly worth studying," she said slyly. "I've got to draw up his chart," she added. "Oh, yes. Can you believe it? My book of Elizabethan spells appeared on the front porch this morning. Isn't that weird? I was so sure Kevin had taken it, but the book was wrapped very neatly in brown paper, and that wouldn't be his style." She chuckled. "You should have seen his face. He was so relieved he was off the hook, he even forgot to argue when I told him he had to clean the attic and basement." She turned away. "I'll see you later, then. And I'll want to hear every detail tonight!" She waved as she moved off.

Holly glanced at her watch. If she didn't leave within the next few minutes, she'd be late to open the shop. It was bad enough she'd have to drive her car to work so she'd have it for her appointment at Mr. Montgomery's. She ran inside for her purse, then back outside to the garage, crossing her fingers that her car would start instead of coughing and spitting as it was prone to do. Another plus for her job was that it was within walking distance, sparing her the daily aggravation of fighting with the wreck.

Like a miracle, the car started right up, as if it understood how important this day was. Even so, she kept her fingers crossed as she backed down the driveway.

Luckily, the morning proved quiet, and Celia arrived promptly at ten. She looked over Holly's outfit, grudgingly approved it and ushered Holly out the door with an annoying last-minute replay of her earlier instructions. Holly was so relieved to be gone, she almost forgot her trepidation over where she was going and whom she was going to see.

"JACK, IF YOU LOOK out that window one more time, I'm going to scream."

He turned from his surveillance of the expansive front lawn, which was now being tended by several groundskeepers. "Someone is coming to look over the clothing in the attic, Ticia. I hope you'll behave yourself."

Letitia glanced in the mirror and straightened the peach silk hairband that echoed the color of her silk T-shirt and calf-length patterned skirt. Even her soft leather flats matched the outfit.

"Mirror, mirror on the wall?" Jack teased.

She looked up, crossed her eyes and stuck her tongue out at him.

"One day you're going to do that and your face will freeze in that expression."

"You're just jealous because you can't cross your eyes and I can."

Jack chuckled at the old argument. "Just do me a favor and don't scare the lady. She seems so shy that one wrong word might send her running."

"Sounds like a wimp."

"No," he said slowly. "Just someone who isn't aware of the power she has. But when she finds out . . ." His head snapped up at a loud sputtering rattling out front.

Letitia glanced out the window and matter-of-factly stated, "The 'lady' drives a car that should have been put out of its misery twenty-five years ago."

"When you're divorced and supporting two kids, you don't always have ready funds for a new car." Then Jack followed the direction of his sister's gaze. "My word, I can't remember the last time I saw one of *those.*"

Letitia frowned as she watched Holly climb out of the old-model vehicle. "How staid. Jack, the woman needs more color to go with that glorious hair!"

He thought of the ginger-colored outfit she'd worn the day before. It had been perfect for her—a redhead with a porcelain complexion. "She did wear the right color yesterday. And looked lovely," he murmured. "I wouldn't be surprised if her boss made her dress that way."

"You did say Celia Parker acted like a regular bloodsucker," she commented. "And the poor woman works for her. Well, you'd better hope Mrs. Boggs doesn't scare her off. I admit this place deserves an ominous housekeeper, but Althea Boggs scared even me. Of course, she can cook like a dream," she added loyally.

Jack turned when he heard the front door open. "I mean it, Ticia, behave. Holly Bennett isn't like the barracudas you and I are used to."

His sister's smile of angelic innocence didn't fool him one bit. "I always behave, brother dear. Like an angel."

IT TOOK ALL HOLLY'S self-control not to climb back into her car and race home. She looked up at the towering edifice before her and shivered. The mansion looked just as forbidding in the daytime as it had the long-ago night Holly, in her junior year of high school, and a few friends crept out here on a dare.

Shoring up what little courage she had, she marched up to the front door and pressed the doorbell, avoiding the weathered brass gargoyle fashioned into a knocker. Utterly spooked, she nearly gasped when the door opened, even though she recognized fellow Salem resident Althea Boggs.

"Yes?" the woman snapped.

"Good morning, Mrs. Boggs. I have an appointment with Mr. Montgomery. I'm representing Celia's Closet."

The housekeeper stepped back to admit her. "Mr. Montgomery is in the parlor." She led the way.

Holly tried not to stare as she traveled down the long hallway, her heels clicking on the polished wood floor. The aroma of lemon oil wafted through the air, and the sounds of hammering and the whine of an electric saw reached Holly's ears. Clearly Mr. Montgomery wasn't wasting any time making the old house habitable.

"Mrs. Bennett," the housekeeper announced at the parlor doorway. She turned to Holly, her pursed lips silently goading her to hurry in.

Holly did just that. "Good morning," she said breathlessly. Her gaze was instantly drawn to the mysterious Mr. Montgomery, but she couldn't miss the lovely woman perched on a tufted window seat studying her as if she was an interesting specimen of a mortal. At a glance Holly's trained eye detected that the woman's outfit would have cost more than most women's entire wardrobe.

"Good morning." The deep baritone did strange things to Holly's blood pressure. "Mrs. Bennett, I'd like to introduce you to my sister, Letitia Danova."

"Half-sister, actually," Letitia drawled, standing and walking over to Holly with her hand outstretched and a warm smile on her peach-glossed lips. "Jack was the product of husband number one, and I was the product of husband number two. After us, Mother gave up on children with the rest of her husbands."

"Ticia, dear, I'm sure Mrs. Bennett isn't terribly interested in our somewhat misshapen family tree."

He couldn't have been more wrong, Holly thought.

Letitia flashed a smile at her brother before turning back to Holly. "So, Mrs. Bennett, you're here to rummage through the attic and sift through some old clothes. Sounds dreary."

"Oh, please, call me Holly. And, actually, this kind of project is rather like a treasure hunt," she admitted, relaxing under the woman's natural warmth. "You're never sure what you'll find."

"Sounds like me when I roam the Paris boutiques." Letitia's laughter rippled like a waterfall. "Would you care for coffee, or something cold to drink?"

"I'd really prefer to get right to work," Holly said, declining politely, and taking great care to avoid looking at the woman's disconcerting brother, who didn't seem to mind looking at her.

Letitia, in turn, looked secretly amused. "Then we'll have Mrs. Boggs take you up to the attic," she said, casting a glance in her brother's direction.

He didn't hesitate. "No, no, I'll escort you upstairs myself, Mrs. Bennett."

"Holly, please," she protested. "And I wouldn't want to take you away from anything, Mr. Montgomery," she said lamely, uncomfortable at the idea of being alone with him for even a few minutes.

"Jack, please," he mimicked kindly. "And you won't be." He took her elbow and headed for the hallway.

Holly hoped he couldn't feel the tremor his touch evoked.

When they reached a wide staircase, he looked at her with concern. "I hope you won't mind climbing three flights."

"No, I don't mind. Actually, I get a lot of exercise walking to the shop since I live so close," she explained as they began their ascent.

Jack guessed it had less to do with distance and more with the state of Holly's car.

"I understand you have children, also. Chasing after them probably helps keep you so. . . fit."

This man could make even motherhood sound sexy, Holly realized. She suddenly felt winded, but not by the steep stairs. "Yes, a girl and a boy," she said, puffing.

She stopped so abruptly that he ran into her back. The feel of his body against her was enough to completely unnerve her. He grabbed hold of her arms before she could lose her balance, and he turned her to face him.

"Sorry, I guess I ran out of breath," she said with convincing breathlessness.

"No problem. Take your time."

Holly stared into his dark eyes, and for one fanciful moment she imagined she saw flames in their depths. Then her attention was caught by a movement on the stairs. A cat. Its fur was the same honey shade as Letitia's hair, and the peach silk collar circling the feline's neck echoed the woman's outfit.

For one crazy moment Holly found herself thinking of witches and their familiars. Lord, what had she gotten herself into? Then, just as quickly, she chided herself for indulging in the fantastic idea. It was all due to Ivy's recent chatter of love spells and missing auras.

"Okay now?" Jack asked. At her nod, they continued up the last staircase, which was considerably narrower. "I'm not sure just what you'll find. When I opened the trunks, I only looked at what was on top. I was afraid to disturb the contents too much for fear of ruining something because I hadn't handled it properly."

Holly began to feel more uneasy on the narrow, dimly lit staircase. Stories of people vanishing mysteriously, never to be seen or heard from again, filtered through her mind. But Ivy and Celia knew she was here, and—oh, she was being ridiculous!

"Here we are." Jack opened a door and walked into the dark interior with the sureness of a cat. "Wait a moment until I turn on a light. Unfortunately, the tiny windows up here are almost nonexistent."

Holly was only too happy to comply. She hovered in the doorway, waiting until Jack found the cord for an overhead light. He stood in the center of the room, smiling at her. She walked inside, and her gaze settled on four old-fashioned trunks set under the eaves.

Jack opened a window to allow fresh air in. "I'll move the trunks into the center of the room for you," he offered.

"No, they're fine where they are. I don't want to keep you from—" She stopped abruptly when he spun around, spearing her with that dark gaze of his.

"Again, you're not." Jack caught the flush staining Holly's cheeks, the way her eyes slid from his. He was right in his assessment: she was painfully shy, almost as timid as her daughter. Well, perhaps she'd loosen up once she knew him better. He fully intended that she know him better. And soon.

He smiled warmly. "Well, if I can't help, then I'll leave you to your 'treasure hunt.' If you need anything, just call out."

Her eyes slid from his to the trunks. "Thank you."

As Jack descended the stairs, he decided to find out all he could about the shy, retiring temptress in his attic. And what better source than Althea Boggs, whose family had lived in Salem for the last two hundred years?

He found the housekeeper polishing furniture. He looked around the large living room, pleased with Letitia's choice. The cream-colored, loose-weave drapes let the sunshine in, and select antiques perfectly complemented the period of the house but were comfortable enough to sit on. There was nothing dark or depressing about the room, and the only touch of stiff formality was Mrs. Boggs, in her black uniform and starched white apron.

"Mrs. Boggs, would you have a minute?" he asked politely.

"I intend to have the downstairs spit-polish clean before I start dinner." Her no-nonsense attitude was what had prompted Jack to hire her.

He settled himself on the couch arm, but when her pale gray eyes fairly sliced through him, he quickly lowered himself properly to the cushions.

"I thought perhaps you could answer a few questions for me...."

"Mrs. Bennett has been divorced for two years. She married Ron Bennett right out of high school, and the boy just plain never grew out of puberty. He was the star of the baseball team, and she was the sweetest girl in school. She was also one of the shyest, probably because of her parents. They were in their late forties when Holly was born, and they tended to keep her close to home. Ron saw something good," she said bluntly, "but once he got it, he didn't know what to do with it. He now coaches the high school baseball team and lives with a young chippie who doesn't have the good sense God gave her. Holly works for that harpy, Celia Parker, at a wage that wouldn't feed a bird, and she's got two kids to support, since Ron's child support checks usually aren't worth the paper they're written on. Holly's daughter, Caroline, takes after her mother by being inquisitive, smart as a whip and just as shy. Ryan is another story.'' Her severe expression lightened a bit. ''Ryan may be only five, but he'd take on the world to protect his mother and sister.''

Remembering that night in the meadow, Jack privately agreed.

''Holly is a lovely woman who needs a good man.'' Mrs. Boggs's glance seemed to assess Jack's potential. ''Someone to take care of her and encourage her inner strength. 'Course, I don't hold with gossip.''

''Of course not,'' he said gravely. His expression remained bland under Mrs. Boggs's fierce scrutiny. ''You don't like me very much, do you, Mrs. Boggs?''

''Don't know you well enough to dislike you,'' she freely admitted. ''You and your sister have some strange ways, but I guess that comes from you living in Europe all that time. I just don't think Holly Bennett needs any more pain in her life. Dealing with Ron is more than enough for any woman, much less an angel like Holly.''

''You seem to know a lot about him.''

As she talked, she continued polishing tables. ''I should. Ron's mother is my second cousin. Myra should have known better than to marry Daniel Bennett. He never was any good. Liked the liquor and the ladies way too much. And the son turned out just like the father.''

Jack had intended to subtly pump Mrs. Boggs about Holly; he certainly hadn't expected this gold mine of information.

''Holly's not the kind to be trifled with,'' the older woman warned.

"Perhaps I could help her overcome her shyness."

Mrs. Boggs stared at him. "You? Why?"

"Because I have no ulterior motive where she's concerned."

She stared at him long and hard. "Yes, you do." She gathered up her cleaning equipment and walked out of the room.

Jack remained in the room for a few moments, inhaling the fresh scent of lemon oil. With its cheerful new trappings, it was hard to believe the house had inspired the ghostly legend of old Humphrey Williams killing himself there and coming back to haunt the place. The legends themselves had appealed to Jack. After all, what better house for him to live in than a haunted one?

He glanced down at his watch. He'd give Holly an hour or so before going back upstairs. By then she'd be grateful for a cold drink and perhaps even his company. Until then, he'd hole up in his office and see if anything would come to mind for his new project.

HOLLY EXAMINED THE contents of the first trunk, then went on to the others. Whoever had packed the clothing had done an excellent job of preserving it. She oohed and aahed over the tea gowns, day dresses and exquisite lingerie carefully wrapped in tissue-thin paper and placed in the cedar-lined chests.

"Oh, my," she breathed, carefully lifting an emerald-green silk ballgown and examining the detailed stitching. Miraculously, its lace trim was separated from the fabric in only a few places.

"How beautiful!"

Holly looked up with dazed eyes to find Letitia Danova standing in the doorway. The woman entered, her eyes on the gown Holly held so reverently.

"And here I expected you to find nothing more than moldy old rags," Letitia commented, touching the low-cut neckline. "I wonder who wore this."

Holly was studying the gown's inner seams. "This wasn't made locally," she murmured. "The work looks Parisian, but I'm not certain."

Letitia looked around at the other items Holly had carefully draped over the trunk lids.

"It's hard to say who would have worn the gown," Holly finally replied. "Despite the macabre legends surrounding Humphrey Williams, all that's really known about him is that he came to Salem in the early 1830s, married the bank president's daughter and built this mansion for her. No one knew exactly how he came by the money to build such a house. There were no children, and rumor has it that on the night of their tenth wedding anniversary, Mrs. Williams ran off with a ship's captain, and Humphrey committed suicide the next day. Legend holds that he had been a professional gambler before he arrived in Salem."

Holly's lips curved in a smile. "Since then, it's been said he walks the meadow on moonless nights and wanders the halls of the home he built for his faithless wife. Many people claim to have seen him."

"But you don't believe it? You, a resident of Salem, Massachusetts, don't believe in ghosts?" Letitia said lightly.

"One of my ancestors was burned as a witch," Holly admitted, "and it's said I'm the spitting image of her. Perhaps no matter where you live, it's hard to know what to believe."

"No wonder Jack finds you so fascinating," Letitia said enigmatically. She eyed Holly slyly. "Jack's a handsome devil, isn't he?"

Unaccountably shaken by Letitia's choice of words, she made no reply. Evidently, her stunned silence was answer enough for the woman.

"I had thought about returning to Europe now that big brother is pretty much settled," Letitia said, "but maybe I'll stay for the summer. It might prove very interesting."

"Ticia, I thought you promised to behave," Jack chided his sister as he walked into the attic room carrying two glasses of iced tea sprigged with mint. "Out."

She grimaced at her brother. "I was just curious, that's all." She walked away with fluid grace.

"Just remember what curiosity did to the cat," he called softly after her.

Tinkling laughter was the only reply.

Holly stiffened. Cat. The peach band around Letitia's hair...the collar on the cat she'd seen earlier. The cat's fur...an exact match of Letitia's hair. Incredible thoughts were once more rolling through her head. Thoughts of witches, warlocks and haunted houses.

## *Chapter Four*

"You'll have to excuse my sister. She tends to open her mouth before she engages her brain." Jack handed Holly one of the glasses. "It's gotten her into trouble before, but she keeps on doing it." He rested his hip against one of the trunks, angling his body in her direction.

Holly sipped the cold liquid, relishing the feel of it trickling down her parched throat. She hadn't realized just how warm and thirsty she was.

"I have a friend who's equally outspoken," she said softly. "I think they enjoy shocking people."

Jack nodded. A little grimly, Holly thought. His attention was diverted to the open trunk beside him. He idly fingered a lace-trimmed chemise. "The workmanship in those days was amazing," he murmured, lifting up the silky garment. Instead of further examining the gown, he gazed directly at Holly. "Lovely."

She could feel her cheeks burn. "I've already made a list of the items I've found so far." She spoke quickly. "And, with your permission, I'd like to photograph some of the gowns. I'm afraid I can't give you a price for the lot, but Celia will go over the list and get back to you." She knew she was babbling but was powerless to stop. What was it about this man that caused this short-circuiting of her brain waves? "Whoever packed the clothing did an excellent job. Admittedly, the muslin has yellowed with age, and lace trims have loosened, but that's not unusual."

"Holly." He moved a step closer.

She automatically moved two steps back. "Celia will kill me for saying this, but you might want to consider donating a few of these gowns to one of our museums. This kind of quality in such good condition is hard to find."

He moved close enough to pluck the tea out of her hand. After setting both glasses aside, he stood in front of her and took hold of her chin in a firm grip. "Holly."

His fingertips seemed to burn her skin. Holly felt her stomach lurch as if she were on a roller coaster. She worked hard to keep her life on an even keel. A man who could unsettle her this easily wasn't what she needed. She dampened her dry lips with her tongue, then instantly regretted the gesture when she saw the dark intensity in Jack's eyes.

"Of course, it's only a suggestion," she whispered.

It was inconceivable that Jack's eyes could get any darker. "I think it's an excellent idea. Which items would you suggest I donate?"

Clutching at the excuse to leave the temptation of his touch, she backed away. "This one." Her fingertip lingered over the green silk gown. "Some of the lingerie, that mauve tea gown. And there's a lovely velvet evening cloak and a beaded bag and slippers in the last chest."

He nodded. "All right. And to save your hide, we won't bother telling Celia. I'm sure she wouldn't care to see her profit drop."

Holly felt compelled to defend her boss. "She's a businesswoman."

Jack smiled. "You're too loyal, Holly. I could see what kind of businesswoman she was yesterday. She should be flattered she has such a loyal employee defending her, but I have an idea she could care less. Have dinner with me tonight."

The change in topic was so abrupt, it took Holly a moment to assimilate the request.

"Why?" she blurted. If she had stopped to think, she would have been horrified at her directness with a man she barely knew. After all, she never even had the courage to confront her ex-husband, whom she knew only too well.

"Because I want you to. You're a lovely woman, we're both free agents. What's wrong with our having dinner together?" Jack asked in a silky tone.

"Because I'm not your type!" she sputtered.

Jack's lips curved with amusement. "Oh? And what is my type?"

"Beautiful, self-assured, cosmopolitan, rich, carefree," Holly guessed accurately. "Not someone working in a consignment shop and trying to raise two children." She raised a hand in a helpless gesture. "I've barely been out of the state, Jack, much less out of the country." She had unconsciously used his first name without his prodding her. That's how unhinged she was.

She had just listed the requirements for the kind of woman he had once sought. But not any longer. He was intrigued with a shy little caterpillar who, he knew, could turn into a bewitching butterfly if given the right encouragement. "The kind of woman you described is often shallow and self-absorbed. Something tells me you think more of others than of yourself. I'm not the party animal you think I am, Holly. I'm new to the area and know very few people, since I tend to keep to myself."

"That's why there's so many rumors about you." She instantly bit her lip. Where was her usual reticence?

Smiling, Jack leaned back, crossing his arms in front of his chest. "Oh? Anything interesting?"

Uncomfortable, Holly grimaced. "People are usually curious about a stranger in town, especially one with the money to buy and restore a mansion like this. All anyone knows is that you've lived in Europe for many years, that you bought the house through a New York law firm... and your company is called Pyewacket. People conjecture about your... occupation. You could be independently wealthy... or you could be old Humphrey Williams come back to life to set Salem on its ear. Or even a vampire or warlock." She finished in a rush and looked up expectantly, hoping he would explain. She was to be disappointed.

Jack chuckled. Wouldn't his people love this kind of publicity! "I had no idea gossip could run rampant so quickly. And what do *you* think?"

"I don't hold with rumors." She tamped down the silent reminder of her own wild imaginings.

He inclined his head. "Then what do you say we give Salem a new rumor to chew on?"

She looked puzzled.

"Have dinner with me."

Holly's laughter was music to Jack's ears. "You don't give up, do you?"

"Never. Perhaps I should just weave a spell around you," he murmured, moving a little closer. "Or keep you prisoner up here until you give in."

Holly's mind conjured up some pretty interesting mental pictures.

"Holly." His serious tone brought her eyes up. "I would never hurt you. I want you to know that. All I'm asking is that you trust me."

If she lived to be a hundred, she knew she'd never again meet a man who tantalized her so easily and made her feel there just might be more mystery to life than she'd thought. "Why is what I think so important to you?"

"Maybe it's you who casts the spells."

She was tempted. Very tempted. But fears still niggled. And the one time she'd dared to date after her divorce had been such a disaster that it didn't bear thinking about.

"It's difficult to get a baby-sitter at such late notice," she improvised softly.

If it wouldn't have been their first time out together, Jack would have suggested they take the children, too. Still, there would be other times. He would have to be patient. He nodded. "All right. Why don't you go ahead and take your pictures, then I'll help you put everything away."

Holly was actually disappointed that he had given in so easily. She pulled the Polaroid camera out of her purse and quickly took the photographs before carefully rewrapping each item. Jack remained silent as they replaced the clothing in the trunks. Then he picked up her purse, led her back down the stairs and ushered her toward the front door. Feeling summarily dismissed, Holly began walking to her car. Then she realized that Jack still had her purse.

She turned and saw him opening the passenger door to his sexy, low-slung black car. He tossed her purse inside. "You aren't finished yet."

Confused, she walked to his side. "I beg your pardon?"

Jack deftly tucked her into the car before she had a chance to protest.

"Don't worry, this is included in the job," he assured her, sliding behind the wheel.

Holly wasn't sure how to react. "*What's* included in my job?"

He half turned in his seat. "Lunch. You've been cooped up in that attic for hours. Now buckle your seat belt, sit back and we're off."

A tiny smile lifted her lips as she obeyed him. After all, the sun was shining, it was a beautiful day, and how many women could resist being kidnapped by a handsome rogue? "Is the kidnappee allowed to ask where we're going?"

He seemed to relax once he realized she wasn't going to put up any further argument. "It's a surprise."

"You don't believe in taking no for an answer, do you?"

"Not when I know the woman involved doesn't really want to say no."

"Jack Montgomery, you are arrogant."

"If not for the arrogance, I wouldn't be where I am today." His teasing gaze sliced in her direction. "Nor would I be sharing a picnic with a lovely red-haired sorceress.''

She shifted uncomfortably in her seat. ''Does that description offend you for any particular reason?'' Jack asked astutely.

''One of my ancestors was convicted of witchcraft. Burned at the stake,'' Holly said quietly, not realizing she was touching the small mole by her lip. ''Legend has it one of the judges lusted after her and convinced himself her witchcraft had ensnared him. He decided burning her would free him of her spell. It obviously didn't work. He killed himself a week after her death. The townspeople agreed he had been cursed by her.''

Jack's mind clicked into overdrive as he considered the possibilities. A woman unfairly convicted and executed. Who better to return and extract vengeance on those who had betrayed her? At the same time, he knew if Holly even sensed what he was thinking, she would run very fast in the other direction. He slowly drove down a dirt road and rolled to a stop at the edge of a grassy, sunlit meadow.

He assisted Holly out of the car before walking to the trunk and pulling out a wicker basket. He led her toward a large tree that afforded shade from the hot afternoon sun. He pulled a blanket from the basket and snapped it out over the grass. He gestured. ''Here you are, madam. Best seat in the house.''

Holly sat down, tucking her legs beneath her. Now that she'd had time to consider her actions, she couldn't believe she'd so readily gone along with his kidnapping scheme. She smiled at her own audacity.

''What's funny?'' Jack asked, observant as ever.

''Private joke,'' she replied enigmatically.

He raised his eyebrows. "Since we're sharing lunch, don't you think we should share the joke?" he said lightly.

"I was just thinking that maybe I'm not such a wimp, after all," she said simply.

"Who said you were a wimp?" he demanded, his expression as thunderous as the devil himself.

She lowered her head, feeling the curls swing across her cheeks, hoping they hid her expression. "It's nothing." She wished she'd stop blurting things out so. What was it about this man that made her do and say things so contrary to her usual nature?

Jack grasped her chin and raised her face. "It was your ex-husband who did this to you, wasn't it? He's the one who forced your inner self into some dark corner it's afraid to leave."

She jerked away from his touch, although she swore she could still feel the heat of his fingers against her skin. "You assume too much."

The fury on his face dissolved into rumbling laughter. Holly was stunned. Jack was laughing so hard, he almost toppled over.

"I don't see what's so funny," she said stiffly.

"You," he chuckled, wiping his eyes with one hand. "I'm sorry, but you sounded so prim and proper that I could have sworn you were a Victorian miss angry with me for daring to be so forward."

A tiny smile tugged at her lips. "I wasn't that bad."

"Yes, you were." He opened a bottle of wine and poured some into a glass, handing it to her.

Holly hesitated, then threw caution to the winds. If she was going to be out of character today, she might as well go all the way. Jack served her crab salad and warm, crusty rolls, all of it as delicious as it looked.

"Tell me about your children," he urged.

The proud mother in Holly didn't need much coaxing. "Caroline is seven, very bright and always ahead of her classmates in school. She loves to read. Unfortunately, she's very shy, and I sometimes worry that she keeps to herself too much." She paused. "Her one dream, the one she doesn't know I'm aware of, is to take ballet lessons." Jack immediately understood the wistfulness in Holly's eyes. Letitia had taken ballet lessons as a child, and he knew the cost was prohibitive for someone in Holly's precarious financial position.

"What about child number two?" he asked quietly.

She smiled. "Ryan is five and the complete opposite of his mother and sister. He would take on the world, if necessary. He's a real scrapper, and, to his mother's dismay, he's been known to battle bullies larger than himself. And win. A month ago a boy in Caroline's class teased her unmercifully, and Ryan overheard. He didn't waste any time butting his head into the boy's stomach and knocking him down. And he told him if he ever said anything nasty to his sister again, he'd do worse next time. I didn't have the heart to punish him," she admitted.

"And what does he dream of?" Jack prompted, although he already knew the answer.

She laughed softly. "Ryan's idea of heaven would be to have a puppy. A neighbor's dog had puppies several months ago, and Ryan wanted one so badly. The trouble is, the pups were half German shepherd, and I knew a dog that size would eat us out of house and home in no time."

Jack deftly speared a peach slice from a container and handed it to Holly. "And what is Holly's dream?"

She bit into the juicy fruit. "To see her children's dreams come true."

He shook his head, bracing an elbow on an upraised knee, his chin resting in his palm. "Admirable. But what does Holly want for Holly?"

She shook her head and said nothing.

Looking thoughtful, Jack deftly changed the subject, asking her about the town and its residents. Finding it easier to talk about anyone but herself, Holly chatted about Ivy and her bookshop, with its ancient and not so ancient texts on all manner of occultism, including magical spells for everything from curing warts to making a disliked person disappear. She told him about Kevin and some of the stunts the eleven-year-old con artist came up with to drive his mother crazy. He laughed at her description of Prudence and Patience Tutweiler, Ivy's aged, identical-twin great-aunts, who firmly believed themselves to be great psychics even though they were usually wrong in their predictions.

"Aunt Prudence insisted the *Titanic* would arrive one day early, while Aunt Patience argued it would be two days late," Holly went on to explain with a smile. "The thing is, they are the sweetest, most generous people in the world, so none of us have the heart to contradict their 'insights.'" She took small sips of her wine. Just being with Jack was enough to tumble her senses into unaccustomed disarray.

"They sound as if they're good people to know," Jack commented, secretly wondering what kind of tidbits they could give him for the work he was planning. Not to mention tidbits about Holly.

"They've lived in Salem all their lives, know pretty much anyone who's been here more than ten years and are a fountain of information about old witchcraft lore," she replied. "Of course, to hear it you have to be ready to sit for hours balancing a teacup in one hand and a plate of sweets in the other. They're delightfully old-fashioned. Ivy's also something of a resident expert on witchcraft, although her expertise comes mainly from books. She's in contact with collectors all over the world, and people serious about magic often visit her shop."

Jack shook his head. "But how can she make any money if she only caters to such an exclusive clientele?"

"She doesn't. Her shop also carries crystals, amulets, herb teas and trendier books on the occult—New Age spiritualism, it's called these days. But her real love is wisewomen lore, knowledge that has survived through generations of paranoia and fear of a subject that seems to defy logic."

"*You* defy logic," Jack said.

She looked up, startled. "How?"

"In a town known for witchcraft and magic, you remain untouched, even though you have the witch's mark." He lightly touched the mole by her upper lip.

"Magic isn't real."

"Says who?"

"Says me."

Jack backed off. Without saying anything more, he applied himself to packing up their plates and glasses. After helping Holly to her feet, he picked up the cloth and shook it out.

Holly felt oddly confused. She freely admitted she was no expert on men, but Jack seemed somehow... different.

"Have you ever been married?" she blurted. Then she gasped. "I can't believe I asked that. I'm sorry. I talk about other people who are too nosy, and then I say something like that."

He grinned. "You've answered my questions. It's only fair you ask a few of your own. Yes, I was married once upon a time. She decided she wanted to be with someone else more than she wanted to be with me, so I knew I should let her go."

He wondered what she would say if he told her the woman he'd thought he would spend the rest of his life with had decided she couldn't live with a man who made the money she loved to spend by dealing with demons. Considering Holly's opinion of magic, he already sensed what she would think of his occupation. He decided to keep it a mystery a bit longer. It just might buy him time to see more of her. He hoped.

"I'm sorry," she said with touching sincerity. "It appears we're both victims of divorce court."

He smiled. "Don't be. She's happier now, and that's what counts." With a guiding hand on her elbow, he steered her back to the car.

"Celia will wonder why it's taken me so long," she said, once settled in Jack's car.

"Tell her you wanted to be precise so she'd be sure to get the best deal. I'm sure that's something she'll understand. Besides, you're entitled to lunch, even if you do work for a slave driver."

"Celia may appear a bit callous at times, but she's an excellent businesswoman," Holly said, defending her boss.

"So I've heard."

Holly knew Celia's reputation in town. While many people didn't like her, they admitted she knew her business. And she'd been savvy enough to hire Holly, who overcame many buyers' reluctance to purchase "pre-owned" clothing by changing a look so completely with accessories that even the original owner could walk in and not recognize her own dress or suit.

"I'm curious about something. Does she have a steady market for period clothing?" Jack asked.

"There are lots of costume balls in Salem, especially around the holidays. And then, of course, there's Halloween. Some outfits she rents out, others are sold outright to collectors."

"Collectors again. Does everyone in Salem have a collection of something or other? What about you?" Jack drove slowly down the dirt road.

Holly grimaced. "Frogs."

He glanced at her. "Frogs? As in if you kiss one it might turn into a prince?"

"Well, not with such high hopes in mind. When I was little, I was given a ceramic frog. I adored it, and my collection began there. So, Mr. Montgomery, if you're to live here, you'll have to begin a collection. What shall it be?"

"Perhaps I'll collect shy little redheads and lock them away in my dungeon."

The words more than caught Holly's attention and she was relieved to see they had arrived back at the house and her car. She needed to escape and mull over the events of the morning.

"Thank you for the picnic. It was very...refreshing," she babbled, out of the car before Jack had even unbuckled his seat belt. "I'm sure Celia will be in touch with you soon." She silently cursed herself for fumbling to find her keys.

"I should be the one to thank you." Jack was out of the car in a flash and had hold of the hand gripping her keys. Before she realized his intent, he lifted the hand to his lips. "Until we meet again, Holly Bennett. Drive safely." He turned her hand so that his slightly open mouth caressed her vulnerable inner wrist. His teeth grazed the translucent skin lightly but firmly enough to send shock waves shooting through her system, making her aware of even more sensitive areas of her body hungering for his touch.

Then he released her, and with his touch still burning her hand, she tumbled into her car, forced herself to concentrate on starting it, silently praised it for catching on the first try and began edging down the gravel drive. It took a lot of self-control not to glance in the rear-view mirror to see if Jack still stood there. She didn't have to look. She could feel him as surely as if he were touching her.

"Who says magic isn't real," she murmured, speeding up once she was out of sight of the large house.

"KISSING THE LADY'S HAND, no less. How continental. You sly dog, you."

Jack watched the dust swirling in the distance. "Letitia, didn't anyone ever tell you you could lose your nose by poking it into other people's business?"

"*You* have, many times, but as you can tell, I still spoke, and I still have my nose." Letitia had come outside and now stood next to her brother. "She's not someone to toy with, Jack."

"That's the last thing I would do with Holly." He was grateful he hadn't told Letitia about the night he'd stopped at the meadow to check out the children fooling around there and had heard two little tykes plead for a father for themselves and a man to make their mother happy. He admitted to himself he had no idea whether he could be that man, but he was tiring of his fly-by-night life-style, and for some reason Salem was tempting him to settle down. And Holly Bennett tempted him as no other woman ever had.

"Your carpenter refuses to enter that last bedroom on the second floor," she announced, following him back inside. "He claims that's where old Humphrey killed himself and anyone who trespasses there invites his own death."

Jack shook his head at the superstition. "Did you go in and prove him wrong?"

"Are you joking? What if he's right?"

"Fine. I'll prove it." He headed for the stairs.

Letitia's teasing voice followed him. "Jack, if you kill yourself, may I have your apartment in Paris?"

"Don't worry, I've already left you this house in my will, and if you expect to get anything else, you'll have to live here for a year."

"You are kidding, aren't you? Jack, aren't you?" Her plaintive voice rose.

"You'll find out after I kill myself, won't you?"

"If you weren't my brother, I'd kill you myself."

It didn't take Jack long to deal with the carpenter. He led the man to the haunted room, entered it, threw open the windows and wandered around.

"Mr. Montgomery, it isn't safe to tempt the fates," the carpenter insisted, looking over his shoulder every few seconds. "While I'm a logical man, there's just some things in this house that don't seem normal."

Jack looked up. "Such as?"

The man shifted uneasily, glancing toward the locked room at the other end of the hall. One of his neighbors claimed he'd driven by one night and seen a strange green light flickering from that upstairs window. Still, Mr. Montgomery wasn't bad to work for, even if he did seem a little strange, what with wearing black all summer long. While exacting in what he wanted, he wasn't difficult to deal with, he promptly paid all bills, and the men's wages were more than fair.

"This house has an old history, Mr. Montgomery," he explained. "There's some of us who don't care to go against it."

"And I wouldn't ask you to," Jack replied patiently. He hadn't missed the nervous looks he sometimes received from the workmen. They weren't sure who—or maybe even what—he was to want to live here. The superstitions appealed to his sense of humor. "I'm sure you and anyone else working in this room will be perfectly safe." He gazed deeply into the man's eyes.

The carpenter stepped back a pace. "Sure, Mr. Montgomery," he said slowly, then turned quickly away.

Jack hid a smile.

"Jack, we might have found a secret passage. You'll have to be the one to explore it." Letitia's lilting voice carried upstairs.

He sighed. "I told Mom I wanted a baby brother. I wish she had listened to me."

# *Chapter Five*

"Give me all the gory details about your meeting with the mysterious Mr. Montgomery." Ivy cornered Holly the moment she parked her car in the garage that evening. She'd had an appointment herself after work, so they'd come home separately. Holly guessed her friend had been standing at her kitchen window waiting for her arrival.

Holly silently agreed with Ivy's description. Jack Montgomery was most definitely mysterious. "He's spending a lot of money to fix up the house," she said out loud. "The downstairs looked lovely—mostly antiques mixed with a few contemporary pieces. I'm sure his sister has a hand in it. She's not at all like him. She's light compared to his dark, and so beautiful you want to hate her but so nice you can't. She's outspoken, while he seems to choose his words carefully." To unnerve a woman until she can't think clearly? "I'm sure you'd like him. He seems awfully interested in magic."

"Perhaps he's looking for a kindred spirit, someone of his own kind," Ivy intoned in a deep voice.

Holly glared at her as they crossed the back lawn which, she noted, needed mowing. "Not funny, Ivy."

"Hey, you have to admit it's all a little unusual," Ivy pointed out. "We're talking about a man of considerable—but mysterious—means who, through a company named for a witch's familiar, buys a well-known haunted house in Salem, Massachusetts. Not to mention that he doesn't have an aura," she finished.

"You want mysterious...." Holly lowered her voice. "After I met his sister, Letitia, I saw a cat that—"

"Was it black?" Ivy interrupted.

"No, its fur was the exact same honey color as Letitia's hair, and it was wearing a silk collar the same color as her outfit."

Ivy looked at Holly. "Are you saying what I think you're saying?"

Holly giggled at their mutual imaginings as they reached her back door. "It gives you something to think about, doesn't it?"

"So tell me what else happened."

Holly looked off into space. "He kissed my hand, and I felt..." She waved helplessly. "I felt as if his touch burned. It didn't hurt, it just..." She trailed off.

Ivy grabbed both hands and inspected them carefully. "No marks. Holly, I hate to tell you this, but I suspect what you felt was pure and simple lust. Of course, there's nothing wrong with that. In fact, for you, it's great," she pronounced. "As for the other, well, let's wait and see what happens, okay?" Ivy was fairly jumping for joy. "After all, there's magic behind any attraction between a man and woman, right?

And Jack Montgomery might be just the man to break whatever spell has been keeping you celibate so long."

"Ivy!" Holly tried to sound outraged, but her lips twitched with laughter at her friend's never-say-die matchmaking attempts. "I thought you said you couldn't see his aura, and that that was a bad sign." It was rare for Holly to get the best of her friend, and she was enjoying every minute.

Ivy was undeterred. "So I look again. After seeing the man, I could even settle for his not having one."

The more Holly thought about it, the sillier she felt. "We sound ridiculous, don't we?"

Ivy smiled. "No, just like perfectly normal residents of Salem."

Holly unlocked her door.

"I'll tell you what. Why don't I come over after dinner, and we'll discus the matter more thoroughly," Ivy suggested.

"All right," Holly agreed, unsure whether she should pursue the subject or not. She pushed the door open.

"Holly?"

She turned around.

"Next time, try for something more than a kiss on the hand," Ivy teased, starting for her own house. "See you about seven-thirty!"

"I FEEL FOOLISH," Holly said when Ivy showed up at the back door carrying a bottle of wine. "You must think I've lost my mind."

"No, just that you're finally allowing your senses to have some say in your life." She walked to one of the kitchen cabinets and pulled out two wineglasses. A rummage through a drawer produced a corkscrew. "I admit I only got a glimpse of the man, but it was enough to start fanciful notions running through *my* mind." She looked around. "Where's the munchkins?"

"Upstairs watching television," she replied. "The last thing I want them to think is that their mother has finally lost her mind."

Ivy nodded. "All right, let's start at the beginning. Describe Jack Montgomery."

"You've seen him. You know what he looks like."

"Humor me."

"Tall—over six feet—black hair, dark eyes, I'd say early to mid-thirties," Holly recited, then stopped as Ivy shook her head.

"I don't want stats. I want to hear your personal impressions of the man."

Holly regrouped. "Thick black hair," she elaborated, "a bit shaggy, but expensively so. Soft-looking, like you'd want to run your fingers through it." She paused. "Dark eyes, but with some kind of light shining deep inside them," she murmured. "Mesmerizing, as if they can delve into your very soul. He's lean, but not thin, like a runner or swimmer. Sleek."

She looked, unseeing, at the far wall, her voice a soft monotone. "A bit of an olive cast to his skin. Maybe a Latin ancestor on his family tree. He walks smoothly, silently, almost as if he could float. A man who's comfortable with his body. He's divorced, and if he spoke the truth, he wishes her happiness. Either he puts on a good act or he's very sincere. He listens as if he's truly interested in what you're saying. He talks very little about himself, but when he does talk, his voice is so hypnotic that you have to listen.''

Ivy was stunned. She was hearing a lot more than she'd expected to hear. Holly Bennett, who kept men at more than arm's length, had allowed a man closer than she thought. ''How did he make you feel?'' she asked quietly.

Holly smiled, still lost in another world. ''Like a woman. A lovely, fascinating woman.'' She suddenly blinked and seemed to return to the present. ''What did you do? What did I say? What happened?'' Her voice rose in agitation.

Ivy studied Holly's troubled expression. ''You really don't know, do you?'' she whispered.

Holly shook her head, looking lost and confused.

''Then I'd say someone ensnared you in a very powerful spell.''

Holly's laugh held no humor. ''That's not funny, Ivy.''

''I'm not trying to be funny.''

She was incredulous. ''Are you trying to say Jack Montgomery had something to do with my suddenly dropping into never-never land? All right, I'll be honest with you. He made me feel things I didn't know were in me, but that shouldn't make me some kind of zombie!''

''Zombies don't feel, remember? You're feeling plenty. You described the kind of man any normal red-blooded woman would kill to get her hands on. Yet you don't remember giving that description. In fact, you looked as if you were in some kind of trance.'' Ivy pushed Holly's wineglass closer to her. ''Here, I think you might need this.''

TWO OTHER SETS OF EARS had also listened to Holly's description—and to Ivy's response.

"See?" Ryan whispered in Caro's ear. "What did I tell you? He *is* made from that magic spell of Kevin's."

"Aunt Ivy's not sure he's magic, and if anyone would know, she would," Caro argued under her breath.

"She said she couldn't see his aura, and she says everyone has an aura. So only magic people don't have 'em," he deduced. "'Cept Mom doesn't understand that she's supposed to fall in love with him and he'll give us a puppy."

"I'm tired of hearing about your stupid puppy," Caro whispered fiercely.

He scowled at her. "We're gonna have to go to his house and talk to him."

Her eyes widened to green saucers. "We can't go there. It's haunted. Billy Pope says his dad says the only reason Humphrey hasn't scared anyone lately is because that man who moved in is Humphrey's friend. Maybe he isn't magic, but a ghost!"

"You can see through ghosts. We couldn't see through him that night," he argued. "Besides, there's no such thing as ghosts, Caro. Mom said so, 'member? Besides," he said with a five-year-old's unerring logic, "Mom told Aunt Ivy she ate with him today, and ghosts don't eat." Ryan stood up and grabbed his sister's hand, pulling her back to her room. "We'll go see him tomorrow," he decided. "We made him up, so he has to do what we want him to."

"All right, smarty pants, but how are we going to get all the way out there without someone seeing us?"

"Kevin will help us. We'll talk to him after day camp tomorrow."

"Kevin won't and you know it."

Ryan was undeterred. "Yes, he will. You'll see."

"MOM'S SPELL BOOK REALLY worked? Awright!" Kevin was alternately fascinated and frightened. He'd seen enough horror movies to know some magic could backfire against the instigator, and he didn't care to get hurt in the process. "So what're you complaining about if you got the guy you wanted?" He concentrated on refitting his bicycle with new tires.

"We need to go talk to him," Ryan explained. "And tell him he's gotta marry Mom soon."

He looked up from his task. "Why? They've got to fall in love first. Just like in the movies."

"Because if we have a new dad, maybe our other one won't come around and upset her," Caroline said softly. "He says horrible things to her, Kevin. She doesn't think we hear him, but we do. He tries to make Mom think she's stupid, and she's not."

Kevin put down his tools. "Yeah, Ron's a real jerk," he stated succinctly. "Mom told Mrs. Powell Ron thinks more with what's between his legs than that sorry excuse for a brain he has."

Caroline and Ryan looked puzzled. "Huh?"

Kevin shrugged. "Hey, you're too young for an explanation, okay? All right, I'll ride with you guys out there, only because if I don't and you go out on your own and our mothers find out, my life won't be worth crap. But I'm not going in that house," he warned. "There's a lot of funny stuff going on out there. If you were smart, you wouldn't go, either. Except," he mused as a thought occurred to him, "if he isn't real, and I can prove it, I could be famous. Maybe get on TV." His eyes it up. "Yeah, okay, when do you want to go?"

"Tomorrow," Ryan said promptly. "Day camp is having a field trip to Sturbridge, and we'll say we can't go. That Mom has something planned for us."

Kevin nodded, impressed with the little boy's devious thought process. "Sounds good to me. Now, get out of here and let me finish fixing my bike," he ordered. The two ran back to their own yard and inside the house.

As he finished replacing the tires, Kevin considered the stories circulating around town about the new resident of Humphrey Williams's house.

"Sure wish I had some infrared binoculars," he muttered, mentally reviewing his collection of military magazines. "Or a night scope. Better yet, maybe I'd better go through Mom's books and find a spell to protect me. Just in case. After all, if I can make someone appear, I should be able to protect myself from him."

"WHAT DID YOU DO, CLEAN out a travel agency?" Jack stared at the pile of colorful brochures littering the table by Letitia's plate.

"I decided I might as well reacquaint myself with the country while I'm here."

Jack selected one at random. "An underground tour in Seattle?"

"It looked like a good place to start. You know, work my way back from the West Coast." She poured herself another cup of coffee. "Mom dragged us all over Europe and refused to come back here except for short visits with Grandma and Granddad, so I don't know anything about our own birthplace. Before I decide where to settle down, I want to know my options," she explained, studying the assorted pastries on a platter before her. "Mrs. Boggs might look like your typical broom-flying witch, but she cooks like a dream. I've probably gained ten pounds."

"You still fit into all your clothes." Jack eyed the slim-fitting slacks and blouse she wore. "And get that cat away from the table."

"You hate my cat," she accused mildly, shooing away the feline who sat stoically by his mistress's chair.

Jack sighed. "It's bad enough you have custom-made collars for that cat to match your outfits." Today, Le Chat's collar was the same watermelon shade as Letitia's blouse. "But he isn't going to eat off my table just because you let him eat off yours."

"He has better table manners than a lot of humans I know. Remember that Belgian duke Mom had to dinner six months ago? The man belched like a steam engine," she recalled with a dramatic shudder.

Jack leafed through the day's mail. He had a letter from his agent along with one from his editor. "They like the ideas," he announced. "I'll have to get down to some serious work right away."

"You mean that idea of the executed witch who returns over the generations to wreak havoc on the descendants of her accusers?" Letitia asked, glancing up when the housekeeper brought in eggs and toast. "Thank you, Mrs. Boggs." She smiled warmly at the grim-faced woman.

The servant merely nodded and left.

Letitia leaned across the table so her voice wouldn't carry. "See what I mean? The woman is made of stone. No doubt she's a certified witch, Jack."

"Rein in the imagination, Ticia. That's my department," he said absently, still reading through one of the letters.

"You haven't answered my question about the witch."

He hesitated. "I'd like to try it, yes. I'm not sure Holly Bennett would appreciate my appropriating her ancestor."

"It's done all the time. Besides, maybe she'll never find out. She doesn't look the type to read horror novels. I only read yours because you're my brother, and because reading them is the only way I can make sure you haven't put me into one of them yet." She shuddered. "And afterward I don't sleep for a week!"

"Good. That means I've done my job properly." Jack picked up a piece of bacon. "I probably will try to work with the idea. My agent loved it."

"She loves everything you write because it makes her rich. You sit in that fortress you call an office, make up horrible creatures, and people pay good money to be frightened to death. It's mind-boggling."

"You forget. My books have only been sold in Europe and the British Commonwealth. They won't be out in the States until next month," he reminded her. "I could flop here."

"I doubt it. Look at the fan letters you've received from Americans who've bought your books abroad. A lot of them have asked how they could get all your other books in the States. Besides, you're single, good-looking and semi-intelligent.'' Her eyes sparkled with laughter. ''Since the majority of book buyers are female, your image could go a long way in jump-starting sales.'' She sighed. ''Too bad Anne Rice practically patented sexy vampires. You could have milked that role. Especially since you always wear black and prefer working at night.''

Jack grimaced. He never enjoyed doing publicity; it was a necessary evil. His publisher was already arranging a promotional tour to coincide with the U.S. release of his first three books.

Letitia returned to her brochures. ''Dinosaur bones? Hmm, I don't think so. Sounds more appropriate for you.''

''I'll be too busy here to think about traveling. And I want to do some in-depth exploration of Salem. I need to get a better feel for the area.''

''People might be shocked to see you walking around in the light of day. Rumor has it you're not even real,'' Letitia teased. ''That you were conjured up during the dark of the moon or something.''

''More like during a full moon,'' he mused.

''You're kidding.'' She studied his face. ''You're not.''

He shook his head. ''I was driving home late one night and spotted three kids in the meadow. I stopped to investigate, and when I got closer I realized they were working on a magic spell. One was a G.I. Joe lookalike drawing a chalk circle and chanting something while a little girl and boy were waiting for a father figure to materialize.'' He toyed with his coffee cup. "The little boy was fighting mad because he figured the older boy didn't know what he was doing, and he was demanding his three dollars back. When I approached them, the older boy looked as if he'd seen a ghost and ran off, leaving the younger ones. What made it worse was that the meadow was suddenly enshrouded in fog, and to them I seemed to walk right out of it."

"Oh, no." Letitia looked concerned. "Those poor babies must have been scared to death."

"They were, especially the girl. The boy had enough guts to stand up to me and, luckily, trust me enough to drive them home. I couldn't leave them there alone. I'd overheard enough to know their father had left their mother for another woman, and they wanted a new dad. The boy especially." He smiled. "So he could have a puppy and a dad to take him to Little League when he got old enough. They'd paid the other kid to use one of his mother's books to conjure up the perfect father. He left it behind when he ran off, so I found out who he was and returned the book." He shook his head in amazement. "Those two were something else to brave the meadow near a haunted house at midnight in the hope that magic would give them a father."

"And?" she prompted.

"And what?" He looked as innocent as he could, which wasn't very.

Letitia punched him in the arm. "What next, big brother? There has to be more to the story, so give."

"Their last name is Bennett."

"As in Holly Bennett?"

Jack nodded.

Letitia's smile broadened. "No wonder you were so interested in the lady. You've been put under a spell meant to have you fall in love with her. Big brother, you don't stand a chance. And to think I was actually considering doing some traveling this summer. Now I know I'll have to stay here and see the outcome."

"Reconsider Seattle, Ticia. You'd be much better off."

"Fall's soon enough for Seattle." Letitia tipped her head when the door chimes echoed throughout the house. "Perhaps that's your bewitched lady now. Do you think that spell works both ways?"

He stood up and tossed his napkin onto the table. "Perhaps it's one of your ex-husbands. I'll get it, Mrs. Boggs," he called out as he walked into the front hall.

"I only have one ex-husband, and you know it, you cretin!" Letitia yelled after him.

Assuming one of the workmen or gardeners had come to the door, Jack was surprised to find Caroline and Ryan Bennett standing on the steps.

"Can't you do this any faster?" Ryan demanded the minute he saw Jack. "I mean, it's not as if Mom's ugly or anything. You have to make her fall in love with you real quick. Didn't Kevin give you enough magic to do it right? We don't have any more money to have him use another spell. Besides, his mom locked up all her books because now she suspects he could have taken the other one even though it got returned." His eyes swept past Jack to see the cat strolling down the hallway. "A cat? I don't want a cat!" he wailed with dismay, spinning around. "Kevin, you stupid creep, you didn't do it right!" he yelled at the figure pedaling furiously down the driveway.

The click of heels behind Jack alerted him to his sister's presence.

"Jack, shouldn't you ask my future niece and nephew to come inside so I can get to know them better?"

## *Chapter Six*

"So tell me, Caroline, Ryan, how did you get all the way out here to the edge of town?" Letitia had immediately ushered the children into the sunlit breakfast room and settled them with milk and pastries.

"I rode with Kevin on his bike, and Caro rode hers." Ryan was evidently the spokesman.

"Does your mother know you're here?" Jack asked.

Caroline shook her head. "She thinks we're on a field trip to Sturbridge."

Jack took the chair next to her. "Caroline..." He spoke quietly; he didn't want to unnerve her any further than she already was. She looked as if one wrong word might make her run. "You're—what—six? Seven?" He tried to recall the ages Holly had given him.

"Seven."

He nodded. "Do you honestly believe I came to life because of your friend's magic spell?"

She lifted her head, displaying the same liquid green eyes he admired in her mother. "Mom says magic isn't real. But she also says if you wish hard enough for something, it might come true. Isn't that a kind of magic?"

"Of course it is." Letitia jumped in. "But it's not the same kind of magic you and your brother had your friend perform in the meadow that night."

Ryan was busy devouring an apple Danish while staring at Letitia. "Are you the cat I saw?" he asked. "I mean, your hair is the same color as his fur, and he had a collar the same color as your blouse."

Letitia wrinkled her nose. "What do you think?"

"Don't make it worse," Jack warned her.

"Ryan's a sensible boy, aren't you, sweetheart?" Letitia smiled at him.

He looked around. "Then where's the cat?"

"Le Chat does what he wants to," she replied.

He looked confused. "*Le* what?"

"It's French for *cat,*" she explained. "Here, let me get you some more milk." She picked up his rapidly emptied glass and disappeared in the direction of the kitchen.

Jack watched her with surprise. "I didn't think she even knew where the kitchen was," he muttered before turning back to Caroline. Looking at her, he wanted nothing more than to gather her in his arms and assure her everything would be all right. For a man who had never given a thought to being a father, he found himself feeling very paternal toward these two. If he didn't know better, *he'd* begin to believe in that magic spell! "Caroline, you'll have to tell your mother you were here," he said gently.

"I know," she said with a sigh. "And she'll be upset with us. I didn't think Kevin could really conjure someone up from one of Aunt Ivy's books, but I hoped that, along with our wishing, it might come true. That Mom would have someone to make her happy. I don't like the way our dad talks to Mom. Aunt Ivy said he tries to make Mom feel stupid because he's the one who's stupid and Mom should just tell him to go to hell, but she said she can't because no matter what, he's still our dad. But he shouldn't do things like that, should he? I mean, they tell us in school we shouldn't ever make somebody feel stupid, so how come he does it?''

Jack was furious that this tenderhearted little girl had a father who clearly didn't deserve her, and that Holly had to put up with the creep. He grappled for an appropriate reply. ''Well, Caroline, sometimes people do things to other people in a misguided attempt to make themselves feel better. Or maybe your dad hopes your mom will go back to him if he makes her think she needs him.''

She shook her head. ''No, Mom doesn't want Dad back, and I don't, either.''

''He said he never wanted us, anyway,'' Ryan piped up. ''We heard him tell Mom.''

Letitia, who had just entered the room, stopped short at his words. Over the children's heads, her stricken eyes met Jack's.

''Kids, Mrs. Boggs asked if you'd like something more than a Danish,'' she said brightly.

Ryan's eyes lit up. ''Pancakes?''

''She'll make whatever you like.''

''Mrs. Boggs is nice.'' Ryan slid off the chair and waited for Caroline to join him. ''And she makes really good blueberry pancakes. We had 'em at a church breakfast once.''

Letitia and Jack watched them leave the room, not speaking until the door swung shut behind them.

"I wonder if Kevin's mother would lend me a magic spell that would turn that sorry excuse of a man into a flea," she bit out. "How could someone be so cruel?"

"*Cruel* isn't the only word." His features appeared carved in stone. "*Stupid, insensitive* and *callous* might fit the bill. Obviously, his favorite target is Holly. She's better off without a bastard like him."

"No wonder those poor little things resorted to witchcraft for a father. They probably thought that was the only way they could find the kind of man they visualized as a father," Letitia went on, tearing her toast into tiny pieces.

"Jack." Her insistent tone prompted him to look up. "You're not showing interest in Holly because of the kids, are you? They're adorable, but you shouldn't pursue their mom for the wrong reasons, no matter how noble. She seems such a nice woman, and, from the sound of things, she's suffered enough already."

Jack thought about big green eyes, wary at first, then gradually sparkling with laughter. A riot of red curls that invited a man's touch. The appealing mark by her lip that invited a man's kisses. "The lady has me thinking a lot of things. Disinterested nobility isn't one of them," he said finally. "I'd like the chance to get to know her better. I think driving the kids back to town will be a good beginning."

"Something tells me she won't be too happy with the children for coming out here."

"No, but they're going to have to tell her sooner or later. It might as well be sooner."

"Jack, are you sure you know what you're doing?" Letitia asked softly.

"No, but I'm learning as I go along."

"MOM'S GONNA BE REALLY mad we didn't go on the field trip," Ryan said with elaborate drama as Jack drove them into town, with Caroline's bicycle stashed in the trunk. "Probably no TV for a month."

"That's if we're lucky," Caroline added and sighed. "You and Kevin always get me in trouble. But I'm the dumb one for going along with it."

Jack chuckled. "You always go along with any stunt they come up with?"

She nodded. "Most of the time. That way I can make sure they don't get into *too* much trouble." She looked up at him. "It was you who left Aunt Ivy's book on her front porch, wasn't it?"

"It looked to be valuable, and it would have been ruined left out in the open."

Caroline giggled. "She told Mom she knew Kevin took it. She just didn't know how it got back all neatly wrapped up, since Kevin would never do that. She was mad at Kevin because she had someone interested in buying the book." She narrowed her eyes as she looked up at Jack, as if searching for something she couldn't see. "Aunt Ivy also said you don't have an aura and that having one is very important. That's probably why she doesn't think you're real. But she thinks you're sexy, anyway."

"At least you're not a vampire," Ryan added. "Vampires can't go out during the day."

"Yes, I've heard," Jack said dryly, steering the car toward Celia's Closet.

"Maybe we're going to get in trouble, but so is Kevin," Ryan announced with bloodthirsty relish. "He took us out there."

"Only because we asked him to."

"He could have said no," he pointed out with his usual logic.

Jack parked in a small lot near the shop and helped the kids out of the car. "Don't worry, I won't let you face your mom alone," he assured them.

"Maybe we shouldn't tell her about the blueberry pancakes," Ryan said slowly.

"Or about trying on Letitia's jewelry," Caro added.

While Jack had attended to some important phone calls, Letitia had kept the children happily occupied until Jack announced it was time to drive into town to see Holly before she learned the children hadn't gone on the field trip and began to worry.

They walked past a shop called Books and Curiosities before turning into Celia's Closet.

"Aunt Ivy's store," Caro explained, pushing open the door.

"I don't know, I've never worn such a bright color before," a woman fretted, staring at her reflection in the mirror while Holly stood nearby.

"But you should, Mrs. Fields," Holly urged, stepping forward. "Look how the color warms your skin tones and even brightens your eyes." She faltered when she noticed Caro and Ryan entering the store with Jack Montgomery right behind them. Dressed in a black short-sleeved shirt and black pleated slacks, he again looked like some dark angel.

She pulled her attention back to her customer. "In fact, I'm sure the same colors would look wonderful threaded through your hair.'' She headed for a rack displaying colorful lengths of silk and rayon. She withdrew two scarves and deftly rolled them to expose shades from both lengths. With the woman's permission, she arranged it as a hairband. ''See the difference?''

Mrs. Fields smiled brightly. ''Holly, you've done it again. I never would have had the nerve to select such a brilliant color.''

''Very lovely,'' Jack quietly pronounced.

Mrs. Fields turned. ''Why, thank you, young man. Hello, Caroline, Ryan.'' She eyed a blushing Holly with curiosity. ''Holly, dear, are you holding back on us?'' she teased. She looked at Jack. ''This girl is a marvel.'' She turned to pat Holly's shoulder. ''You should have your own shop, dear, where you'd have completely free rein.'' She lowered her voice. ''There's a good many of us who only come in here because of you. Not for that witch, Celia.'' She headed off to the dressing rooms.

Holly hurried over to the trio. ''What happened?'' she demanded in a voice laced with panic. ''Why are the children with you?''

''That's a long story,'' Jack replied, admiring her sunny appearance in a golden-yellow blouse worn partially open over a dull orange T-shirt and tucked into dark tan slacks.

She bit her lip and turned to Caro. ''You were supposed to be on a field trip to Sturbridge today. You'd better have a darn good explanation, because right about now I'm not very happy with you.'' She sighed. ''I guess you'll have to stay here in the shop until I close.''

Jack saw his chance and grabbed it. "Actually, I was going to ask you if they could tag along with me while I tour the town," he said. "That is, if you don't mind. I'd be sure to keep a close eye on them. That way, you won't have to worry about them, and they'll get a bit of a history lesson along the way."

Both children looked up with hopeful faces.

"Please, Mom?" Caro pleaded, jumping up and down.

"I promise to be good if you let us go," Ryan begged, grabbing hold of her leg.

"There's something not right here." Holly peered at Jack, trying hard not to drool. Did he always have to look so good? "They should be on a field trip with their day camp, yet they show up here with you. That's grounds enough for punishment, and you're talking about giving them a treat? No, I'm sorry. I can't allow it."

"Be honest, Holly. Trying to keep them quiet here in the shop all afternoon won't help your peace of mind any," Jack pointed out. "I promise to keep an eye on them and have them back by closing. I do want to see the sights of Salem, and this way you won't have to worry about them."

She could feel those dark eyes snaring her senses again, and, as before, she was powerless against their power. "I should say no...."

Both children sensed her weakness, as did Jack, but he wasn't about to push it. He wanted her to make the decision on her own, rather than feel manipulated.

She sighed. "You're right." She looked back and noticed Mrs. Fields exiting the dressing room. "Wait here." She hurried back to the counter to write up the sale.

"A handsome gentlemen," Mrs Fields remarked. "Is he new to the area?"

"Yes, he is. Mr. Montgomery purchased the Williams property," Holly answered as she totaled up the items and accepted the woman's credit card.

Mrs. Fields's eyes widened. "He's the one?" She turned her head, staring at Jack, who returned her intense gaze with one of his own. Flustered, she quickly turned back and scribbled her name across the charge slip. She practically snatched the bag out of Holly's hands and rushed out of the shop.

"Has my deodorant lost its power?" Jack quipped.

"More like all the rumors running around town about you," she muttered, opening her purse and pulling out her wallet.

Jack frowned. "What are you doing?"

"This is for the kids. Ryan especially believes he might starve every two hours or so." She withdrew several bills.

Jack's hand whipped forward and clamped down on her wrist. "Put it away. I can afford whatever they want. As it's my idea, it's also my treat. Or have you changed your mind about my taking them?" His quiet voice was so forceful, she hesitated. She sensed what he was really asking. After Mrs. Fields's reaction, he assumed she might feel the same mistrust.

"For some reason, the kids feel comfortable with you, and since you obviously don't mind baby-sitting them, I guess it's all right for now. But I do intend to hear the entire story when you bring them back. And they have to understand that their going out this afternoon doesn't mean they won't be punished.'' She gazed long and hard at each child.

''No TV for a month,'' Ryan predicted glumly.

''I'm glad to see you recognize the consequences for lying,'' Holly said gently but firmly.

''Come on, let's get out of here before you make matters worse.'' With a hand on each child's shoulder, Jack guided them out the door.

Holly watched them leave. Not until they were outside on the sidewalk did she realize the bells over the door hadn't rung, although they had when Mrs. Fields left just a few minutes before.

''How does he do it?'' she murmured.

''This is incredible.'' Ivy ran into the shop, the bells over the door tingling madly at her entrance. ''What on earth's going on?''

Holly merely shook her head in resignation. ''For some reason the kids didn't go on the camp field trip today but ended up with Jack Montgomery, and he brought them here. More than that, I don't know, and it appears I won't find out for a few more hours. He's visiting some of the town's tourist areas, he assured me he would enjoy their company, and he promised he would take good care of them. And, deep down, I know he will, even though I know so little about the man. Would you like to tell me now I'm crazy or wait until later?'' She paused to take a much-needed breath.

Ivy shook her head. ''I was right the first time.''

''That I'm crazy?''

Ivy shook her head. ''No, you're as sane as any woman wildly attracted to a gorgeous man can be. What I'm talking about is that the man doesn't have an aura. When he and the kids walked past my shop, I got a much better look at him than I did the first time. His aura is a perfect blank! No color, no form, no nothing! Something is not right." She tapped her forefinger against the counter for emphasis.

While Holly adored Ivy, she found it difficult to believe in auras, psychic readings, Tarot cards and the strength found in crystals. Though she sometimes still wished she could believe that magic might change a person's life, she had learned the hard way that magic just plain didn't exist. Especially the kind of magic she had once hoped for.

"Ivy, if only things could be so simple," she said and sighed. She began neatening the jewelry display.

Ivy shifted gears and smiled slyly. "You know, I wonder what good old Ron will think of Jack Montgomery's attentions to you. Wanna bet he'll play a real dog-in-the-manger when he hears another man's coming on to you?"

"You forget, Mr. Montgomery's attention is directed toward my children, not myself." Holly could feel the blush burning her cheeks. The same kind of burn streaked across her wrist. The wrist Jack's lips had caressed.

Ivy shot her a knowing look. "I'm going to have to do some research on people without auras. There has to be an excellent reason he doesn't have one."

"Such as everyone's assumption he's some kind of demon friend of Humphrey Williams's, or that he's a reincarnation of the old Humphrey himself?"

"I went to the library to find a picture of Humphrey," Ivy told her. "The man was so ugly, no wonder his wife ran off with another man. If Jack

Montgomery is a reincarnation, someone did him a wonderful favor in his present life. Hey—" she laid her hand on Holly's arm "—relax, okay? I'm the first to admit I go off the deep end sometimes."

"It's because none of us knows anything about the man," Holly replied. "And, as so many of us seem to enjoy doing, we start imagining things that aren't there."

"Then I guess it's up to you to find out the truth. My, my, I envy you your mission." Ivy grinned. "I'll see you later."

Holly spent the afternoon alternately waiting on customers and glancing at the clock. She still couldn't believe she had allowed a man she barely knew to take her children sightseeing! What was it about him that inspired such trust? One thing she intended to do was find out how he managed to short-circuit all her sane thought processes. Not to mention inspire such ease in her normally suspicious daughter. Caro wholeheartedly took to the talks about staying away from strangers, yet she had actually begged to go along with Jack. A man she really didn't know! Holly could feel a headache coming on.

"MOM, MOM, WE WENT to the Witch Museum!" Ryan galloped into the store, skidding to a stop in front of his mother. "And we saw the witches on trial, and we went to the dungeon where they kept them. It was spooky."

"He also belched after he drank a Coke and laughed 'cause he thought he was being funny," Caro said derisively. "He acted just like a baby."

Holly's gaze floated over Ryan's and Caro's heads to Jack, who was right on their heels.

"I enjoyed the afternoon immensely," he said without a trace of guilt.

"I hope they weren't too much trouble," she asked.

"On the contrary, it was fun to see the town's history through their eyes," he answered.

"And we saw Aunt Prudence and Aunt Patience." Ryan tugged on Holly's hand. "Aunt Prudence says Jack was a highwayman in England three hundred years ago. Jack says a highwayman is like a robber, but I told him Aunt Prudence has trouble getting things right. And Aunt Patience told Aunt Prudence she needed to go back on her medicine 'cause she didn't know what she was talking about. She says Jack is a warlock. I told them they're both wrong, he's just made from magic."

Holly stiffened. "What?"

Ryan edged away a few paces. "We didn't do anything wrong. And Aunt Ivy got her book back."

Holly's gaze moved from Ryan to Caroline, who refused to look at her, to Jack, who wore an enigmatic smile. "What are you talking about?"

"Why don't we discuss if over dinner?" Jack said easily.

"Pizza!" Ryan shouted.

"I was talking about your mother and me. Perhaps your Aunt Ivy would look after you two," he said.

"It doesn't matter. We're still in trouble," Caro said dejectedly.

"I—I have things to do," Holly said, refusing his invitation.

"Such as?" He called her bluff.

She wasn't about to lie, especially in front of her own children. "All right. My chores can wait. But I'll have to ask Ivy." She telephoned the bookshop. She wasn't surprised that Ivy readily agreed to feed Caro and Ryan dinner. She even suggested Holly send them next door right then, saying they could help her put out a new shipment of books she'd gotten in that day.

"It won't take me long to close up," Holly told Jack once the children ran next door.

Except it took her longer than she expected because her fingers refused to listen to the dictates of her brain as she tallied the bank deposit, counted out the cash and locked the rear door.

"Do you believe what the others are saying about me?" Jack's fingertips on her shoulder stopped her short.

She glanced over her shoulder, surprised by the abrupt question. "I'm not sure I know what you mean," she evaded.

His dark eyes bored into hers. "Do you believe I'm a product of magic, sent here to seduce your soul?"

Seduce, yes. If it was to be her soul, she wasn't sure. Either way, Holly said nothing.

# *Chapter Seven*

Jack swung his car into traffic as Holly gave him directions to one of the town's most popular restaurants. She decided this was as good a time as any to see what she could learn about the man. "I know you lived in Europe, but were you originally from Massachusetts?" she asked, fishing for information.

"Actually, I was born in Connecticut. My mother's third husband was British, and we moved to London when I was twelve. Right now, I have a very nice farmhouse outside of Paris," he replied, taking a side street Holly indicated. "My mother still lives in London, and Ticia's main residence was in Rome until her divorce. She's staying with me until she decides where she wants to live next."

"You're very lucky to have had the opportunity to do so much traveling." She couldn't keep the envy from her voice.

"Some people travel because they haven't found what they want yet," he explained. "Once they find it, they don't need to search anymore." He pulled into the restaurant parking lot, climbed out of the car and walked around to assist Holly out. When they reached the entrance, Holly paused, her attention caught by something across the street.

Jack followed her troubled gaze. A man was watching them with narrowed eyes, while a pouting young woman in tight shorts and a halter top pulled on his arm and appeared to be saying something.

"Someone you know?" Jack asked.

Holly swallowed a choking laugh. "My ex-husband and his girlfriend."

Jack draped his arm around her shoulders and turned her back toward the restaurant. "They'll have to settle for being on their own. I want you all to myself this evening."

Once they were seated, Holly observed, "You're a very take-charge person, aren't you?"

He shrugged. "Comes from years of practice."

"Yes, I assumed that after seeing the way you handled things today. When do I hear the reason Caro and Ryan were with you instead of on their field trip?"

Jack had hoped he'd have more time to sort out his story. If he told Holly the whole truth, she might be embarrassed to find out how much her children knew about her miserable relationship with her ex-husband, instead of feeling flattered that they loved her enough to try anything to make her happier.

"Can't we save the serious talk for after our meal?"

Her face fell. "Is it that bad?"

"No," he said easily. "But that way I can pretend I'm simply out to dinner with a lovely lady."

"Lovely! My hair is too curly, I'm skinny, and I have freckles even makeup can't hide! Lovely, you say?" She scoffed.

"Your hair is like wavy copper fire," he said quietly, "your eyes like liquid emeralds. A lot of men like freckles, and you're slender, not skinny. You must listen to all the wrong people."

"You certainly have a way with words," Holly said wryly. She looked up when the waiter approached them for their order. She settled on a lamb dish, while Jack chose rare prime rib.

"Thank you," he said enigmatically. "I do like words. Speaking of which, your kids are great, and they're both quite articulate for their ages."

"They both learned to read early on." She warmed under his sincere praise. "Caro always preferred to read books herself instead of being read to, and she quickly picked out words. Now she helps Ryan with his reading. I consider their intelligence above normal, but I'm their mother, so I guess I could be prejudiced. As for Ryan's interest in the more gruesome aspects of Salem's history, I'm not totally surprised. I'm sure the next step will be bringing home lizards and frogs." She smiled. "I'm not sure I'm ready for that stage."

"I doubt any mother is. Mine couldn't understand why I wanted a python for my tenth birthday. She tried to talk me into a new bike instead."

Holly wrinkled her nose in distaste. "I don't blame her. I don't think I'd be too happy if Ryan wanted a snake."

Jack's smile warmed his dark features. "She wasn't too pleased when my stepfather gave me one. He told me I would have to take complete responsibility for Albert, including feeding him live mice."

Holly was horrified. "Live mice?"

"That's what you can look forward to."

She made a face. "Not if I can help it."

Jack leaned back in his chair and surveyed Holly, gratified to see she finally felt comfortable in his presence, no longer looking as if she'd bolt at any second. She smiled up at the waiter as he placed their appetizers before them.

"I have to admit I'm very hungry," she confessed. "I didn't have time for lunch today."

"You wouldn't have any excuse if you had Mrs. Boggs around. She firmly believes in three meals a day, and snacks in between. Of course, then she grumbles about being overworked in the kitchen. Still, she refuses all offers of getting her more help," Jack said, munching on a stuffed mushroom. "Ticia's complaining she's putting on weight and needs to look into a health club. Which says a lot, since my sister's idea of exercise is shopping."

"You two are very close," Holly observed.

"Friends as well as siblings," he acknowledged. "We've always been there for each other."

Holly chewed thoughtfully on a crispy potato skin garnished with melted cheese and bacon. "That's the way Caroline and Ryan are. I just hope they don't drift apart."

"I don't think you'll have any worries on that score. Despite some healthy competition at times, they seem to get along famously." He chuckled. "They were both a lot of help in getting around town."

"I'm sure you know you're the object of curiosity around here," she said casually.

"I received a few strange looks today after Ryan, oh, so helpfully, told people I bought the Williams estate. Ryan told me most folks wouldn't even venture near the property because of Humphrey's ghost."

"It's a rite of passage for teenagers to go out there at midnight on the anniversary of his death in hopes of catching a glimpse of him stalking the meadow or the house," she admitted.

Jack shrugged. "Well, if Humphrey doesn't mind my buying his house, I don't mind sharing it with him."

"You mean if you had known about him in the beginning, you still would have bought the house?"

He tried a fried zucchini strip next. "Naturally."

Holly wasn't sure what to think now. What kind of person would willingly share a house with a ghost, unless... She mentally shook her head. No, Jack was every bit as human as the next person. She looked up to find him studying her with that intense gaze of his. Then again, no other person made her feel as unsettled as he did with just the arch of an eyebrow.

"You're thinking too much again." His quiet voice effectively penetrated her ruminations.

"How do you do that?" she demanded, fearing what else he might learn if he decided to probe her thoughts.

"Do what?"

"Read minds?"

He smiled. "I learned a long time ago not to give away all my secrets."

Holly was relieved when the waiter reappeared with their entrées.

Jack was lavish with horseradish. "I like food with a bite to it," he explained. His teeth flashed white in the candlelight as he smiled.

For one brief second Holly imagined his canines growing just a tad and glistening with an unearthly light. She quickly looked down at her meal, trying to banish thoughts of those same teeth feasting on her neck.

"This is definitely an improvement over McDonald's," he said, cutting into his blood-rare meat.

She chuckled. "Obviously, you indulged my kids."

"Caro prefers 'Mickey D's' to Burger King." He paused. "When she told me I could call her that, I gathered I had met with her approval."

She liked his sensitivity. "Yes. She only lets close friends use the family nickname."

"It must be hard for you at times. Your work, the kids, trying to keep it all together without your ex-husband's help." He shrugged under her startled look. "Blame Patience and Prudence for going on about 'that horrible Ron, who cares more about that harlot than about his own dear, sweet children.' Prudence insisted that Ron would eventually learn the error of his ways, while Patience kept muttering something about boils and warts."

"As none of their predictions has come true yet, I don't think Ron has anything to worry about," she said wryly. "They're darlings, though, and they have only the best intentions."

"Yes, I gathered that their prophecies were a tad off base when Prudence assured me my brother wouldn't require his operation, after all."

A smile tugged at the corners of Holly's lips. "Did you tell her you don't have a brother?"

Jack shook his head. "I didn't have the heart."

They finished their dinner with rich, dark coffee. Holly's earlier unease disappeared as Jack shared anecdotes of traveling with a mother who couldn't read an airline schedule or map to save her life. As a result, one summer trip to Crete turned into a month in Portugal.

"Ticia and I were never sure where we might end up, but Mom always made it an adventure," he told her.

"What does she do now that you and your sister are grown?"

"She lives in London and is married to a very nice barrister who knows how to read maps and airline schedules," he explained.

"If you have a house in France, your sister has one in Italy, and your mother lives in London, why would you decide to settle down on the other side of the ocean? And not even in a large city."

"I'm not mad about cities. I prefer to keep to myself for the most part," he answered, deftly avoiding her first question.

"And you prefer haunted houses?"

"And women with freckles and hair like fire." His husky voice swirled through her mind like smoke.

Holly set down her coffee cup with a clatter. "I think it's time I got home to the children," she said.

Jack knew enough to back off. "All right." He signaled the waiter for the check, paid the bill, then escorted her outside.

During the drive home, Holly was quiet, inspecting her feelings. Jack hummed a tune under his breath. At the house, she practically leaped from the car.

"Thank you so much for dinner," she said breathlessly over the top of the car as he climbed out. "Sorry to cut it short, but I don't like to take advantage of Ivy."

Jack knew there was more to it than that. Holly was unsure of what was happening between them, and she was frightened by that. So frightened that she'd forgotten her reason for seeing him tonight.

"I'll see you to the door," he insisted.

They moved up the walk side by side, Jack once more humming the tune under his breath.

"Again, thank you for a lovely dinner," she said formally as she unlocked her front door.

The porch light illuminated his wry smile. "As several of your neighbors are watching from behind their discreetly parted curtains, I won't embarrass you by kissing you good night the way I want to. We'll save that for next time." Before she could react to his comment, he picked up her hand and laced his fingers through hers, the decorous intimacy just as seductive as any kiss he might have given her. "Good night, Holly. Until next time." As before, he raised her hand, palm upward, to press his lips against her inner wrist. And, as before, the touch sent seismic tremors along her nerve endings. "One suggestion. Exchange that hundred-watt bulb for twenty-five. We'll have more privacy that way," he said as she rushed inside.

It wasn't until the door closed behind her and she heard the muted roar of Jack's car pull away from the curb that she realized she'd never even heard the story of what had happened that day! Oh, Lord, the man was definitely dangerous.

"Tell all. How does he kiss?"

Holly spun around. The muted murmur from the television set had muffled Ivy's approach.

"He didn't kiss me," Holly blurted.

Ivy's mouth dropped open. "What? He didn't even try? Even a man without an aura should do better than that."

"He—he didn't want an audience." Holly wished she could call back the words the moment they were spoken.

Ivy's eyes gleamed with understanding. "Oh, yes. Mrs. Hudson usually spies on everyone with those high-powered binoculars of hers. Then there's Mrs. Moore, who's convinced anyone who doesn't live on the block is a potential burglar, and Miss Curtis, who's just plain nosy. Plus, there's that bright porch light of yours. If I'd thought about it, I would have left it off." She made a face. "I may as well get the bad news out of the way."

Holly groaned. "What did they do now?"

"No, the kids were great. But Ron called."

"Damn," she muttered as she tossed her purse onto a chair. "We saw him with Eileen when we arrived at the restaurant, and he didn't look happy."

Ivy nodded. "What did I tell you? Seeing you out with another man probably pricked his overinflated ego. Want some advice from a well-meaning friend?"

Holly dropped onto the couch and rubbed her aching temples. "If I say no, will the well-meaning friend remain silent?"

"No."

She sighed. "I didn't think so. Go ahead."

"Don't return Ron's call. You've obviously got a headache. Why make it worse by listening to him rant and rave? And you know he will. He likes to control people and things, Holly. He always has. And right now, you're showing him that he no longer has any control over you. But if you call him back tonight, he'll figure he does. Don't give him the satisfaction. He was the one to walk away. He shouldn't be allowed to control a family he threw away like last week's garbage."

Holly moaned. When had life become so complicated?

"Holly, honey, you're too young to lock yourself away from the opposite sex. And Jack Montgomery is a magnificent male specimen for you to practice on."

"The man is lethal."

Ivy frowned. "Maybe he's a Gemini. Gemini men tend to follow the dictates of their minds before their hearts. That would explain why he was cautious on the porch."

Gemini. The twins. The idea of Jack leading a double life wouldn't surprise Holly one bit.

"It's all so crazy," she sighed. "And more craziness is the last thing I need in my life right now. Did the kids say anything about why they didn't go to camp today?"

"Something about wanting to see the haunted house," Ivy replied. "And Kevin, who will be suitably punished, agreed to take them out there."

Holly shook her head. "I don't understand any of it. They've never done anything like this before. Ivy, if they suddenly turn into juvenile delinquents, I know I won't be able to handle it."

"Sure you will," she assured her friend. "Besides, I don't think you need to worry. Who knows, maybe one of their friends dared them to go out there. But speaking of juvenile delinquents, I'd better get back to mine and see if he's left anything intact. I don't like to leave him alone too much these days, but I didn't want to keep your kids up too late, so we came back here to tuck them in."

On her way to the door, Ivy stopped. "You know, after listening to Caro and Ryan sing Jack Montgomery's praises all evening, I decided to give him a second chance. I also went through my books for information on a person without a visible aura. It isn't mentioned anywhere. So, who knows, maybe it's a good sign." She headed for the door. "I'll see you tomorrow morning."

"Thanks for looking after the kids on such short notice."

"Are you kidding? They're a pleasure after dealing with Kevin and his crazy notions lately." The door closed behind her.

Holly turned off the lights and went upstairs with the idea of relaxing in a bubble bath. As she began running the water into the tub, she realized she was humming the same tune Jack had. Like a bolt of lightning the catchy tune's title came to her. "Bewitched, Bothered and Bewildered." How fitting!

KEVIN WAS ON A MISSION. After leaving a lump of clothing under his bedcovers in case his mom looked in on him, he set off on his bike. He'd seen Jack Montgomery drive away from Holly's house. He wasn't worried about keeping up with the powerful foreign car. The man was probably heading home, anyway.

Kevin just wanted to see if the rumors were true about the strange lights coming from the house late at night. By the time he reached the mansion, Jack's car was obviously put away for the night.

He crept around to the rear of the house, grateful for the thick shrubs that hid him from view. He peeked in a lit window and saw Jack pour himself a drink and talk to a blonde. The sister. Odd how two people could be related and not look like each other. After a while the pair left the downstairs room, and within moments two things happened. First, the strange glowing light appeared in an upstairs window. Then an outside light came on, and the back door opened to allow a cat to saunter outside.

"I knew that guy wasn't real," Kevin muttered. "And neither is the sister." The cat looked remarkably like the woman he'd just seen through the window. Same hair color and everything. And it was wearing a collar the exact same color as the outfit he'd seen on the woman. "Mom's books work better than even she knows. I musta conjured up a real warlock *and* a witch from that book." He straightened up. "And it's up to me to make sure the guy goes back to wherever he came from before he starts drinking blood or beaming innocent people off to another planet." That he was mixing horror with science fiction didn't bother him. He was too busy seeing himself as the town hero. He'd show everyone just how haunted the Williams house really was.

# *Chapter Eight*

"Holly, dear, how are you?"

It was only eleven in the morning, and her smile already felt stiff from all the people who "just happened to drop by."

"Aunt Prudence, Aunt Patience." She turned from the mannequin she was outfitting to greet the two elderly ladies clad in identical lilac floral dresses with matching amethyst brooches pinned to their lace collars. Straw hats, spotless white gloves and white purses completed their summer ensembles. When Holly hugged and pecked each lady on the cheek, she detected the familiar scents that individualized each woman. "What brings you in today?"

"Your young man."

She looked wary. "My what?"

"Your young man. Isn't that right, Patience?" Prudence turned to her sister, whose head bobbed up and down. "We met him yesterday when he and your children came out of the museum. Such a well-mannered young man, and he handles your little ones beautifully." She wagged a finger at Holly. "Don't let such a fine catch get away from you, dear. I just know he'll find an excellent position in a large corporation where he'll be making a good salary. He's a hard worker, mark my words. I realize he's worried about his brother right now, but I assured him there's no need.'' She patted Holly's arm.

The last time Aunt Prudence had declared a man was a solid, hard-working citizen, it turned out he was a con artist working a cross section of eight states, swindling little old ladies out of their pensions.

''Oh, no, sister, clearly Mr. Montgomery is a man of great logic, a scientist,'' Patience corrected her sister. ''He is clearly the type who prefers to putter around a laboratory all day rather than shut himself up in a stuffy office.''

Holly had to stifle a smile. ''Actually, Mr. Montgomery hasn't mentioned his occupation.''

Both women nodded. ''He's shy.''

Holly coughed to cover the laughter bubbling up her throat. Jack, shy. The man scorched her nerve endings just by looking at her with those midnight eyes. Thanks to him, after a bubble bath that had done nothing to soothe her, she had spent a sleepless night, which had left her unusually grumpy this morning. Her children had left for day camp with relief etched on their faces. And she still hadn't found out why they had gone all the way out to Jack's house.

Patience lowered her voice. ''Celia isn't around, is she?''

''No, she's visiting friends in Maine. She's due back today or tomorrow.''

''I just know she was a spoiled Southern belle in New Orleans before the Civil War,'' Prudence pronounced. "She has that way about her of expecting everyone to wait on her hand and foot."

Patience shook her head. "Pru, I've told you time and time again, Celia was a courtesan in Rome who only entertained senators. And over the centuries she's never lost her haughty manner. Or her hunger for men."

Holly looked down, fearing she would burst out laughing. "Celia brought in a lovely collection of antique handkerchiefs a few days ago. They're very fine linen, with beautiful handmade lace edging and embroidery. Would you care to see them?" she asked, indicating the display in a glass case.

"Carrying a handkerchief is the sign of a lady," Patience agreed as she bent over the case. "Those horrible paper tissues are barbaric. Oh, Prudence, look at that beaded bag in the corner. Doesn't that look like Mattie's?"

Holly kept silent. Prudence was correct. Mattie Chase, a soft-spoken lady also in her eighties, lived on a fixed income that she occasionally extended by bringing in some of her possessions on consignment. Holly felt sorry for the woman, because she knew the lovely purses and costume jewelry were dear to her.

"Yes, it does look similar, doesn't it." Prudence's sharp eyes met Holly's bland gaze. "May I have a closer look at it, Holly?"

She unlocked the case and pulled out the beaded bag, laying it on the glass top. Prudence picked it up carefully and looked it over. That none of its jet and silver beads were missing and that the silk lining was in excellent condition attested to the care the owner had given it. Prudence glanced at the price tag before handing it to Holly. "I'll take it. But I still want to see those handkerchiefs. Good handkerchiefs are impossible to find nowadays."

Patience chose two silk scarves and wandered off to look at the jewelry while Prudence added four handkerchiefs to her purchase and waited for Holly to add up their bill.

"Has Mattie brought in anything else?" Prudence asked softly.

"Mattie comes in occasionally," Holly said hedging.

"Holly, dear, please don't lie to me. I know she has financial troubles and has had to give up some of her precious belongings. I also remember the day her fiancé gave her this bag. He was killed in an automobile accident, you know. She wouldn't give up something this dear to her unless she absolutely had to."

"You can't just give it back to her." Holly spoke quietly. "She doesn't want anyone to know about her troubles."

"Yes, I know her pride very well. But her birthday is coming up next month. I'll tell her I found a twin to her old bag and couldn't resist picking it up for her."

Holly smiled. "Aunt Prudence, you're as much of a softy as Aunt Patience."

The older woman looked down her nose. "That is one trait I would not care to share with my sister. She brought in another stray cat yesterday. As if there aren't enough! I told her that just because old women are known for allowing cats to overtake their lives doesn't mean we have to keep up the tradition. After all, these are enlightened times, and women, no matter their age, can do whatever they're best at. Since we have such clear insights into the future, rather than dallying with pussycats, we must concentrate on sharing our wisdom with others. To help them properly plan their lives, you understand."

Holly arranged her features in a noncommittal mask. If anyone ever used the Tutweiler sisters' predictions to plan her future, she'd be in big trouble! "Of course."

"You just concentrate on that dear Mr. Montgomery. He would make a wonderful father for Caroline and Ryan," Prudence sagely advised. "I realize the poor man is shy, but perhaps the love of a good woman will bring him out. Some men need that kind of emotion to release their true inner powers." She pursed her lips. "Although I do wonder if the man might not have a few more powers than we mortals are meant to. Still, he is devilishly handsome."

Perfect choice of words, Holly thought again. "I scarcely know the man, Aunt Prudence."

Prudence wrote out a check and handed it to Holly. "Holly, my dear, we love you very much, but you must consider the children. You'll be turning thirty before you know it, and it will be more difficult for you to attract the right kind of man. At least Mr. Montgomery is nothing like Ronald." Her features tightened. "I remember when he was born. Patience was certain he would grow up to enter politics. I never shared that view. I always knew he would come to a bad end. Apparently I was right, since he's living in sin with that little tart with the bleached hair and false fingernails." She patted Holly's hand. "Don't worry, everything will turn out fine." She kissed Holly's cheek and gestured to her sister. "Hurry up, Patience, or we'll be late for the Garden Club meeting. And you know how testy Winnie gets if we don't start on time."

Once the two ladies had left the shop, Holly groaned, burying her face in her hands. "What next?"

"Holly, are you out there?" one of her worst nightmares called out from the rear of the shop as the back door slammed shut.

"Yes, Celia," she muttered under her breath, and quietly added, "Where else would I be?" She raised her voice. "You're back early."

"I got so bored up there," she drawled, strolling into the main part of the shop. She held up the packet of photographs Holly had given her just as she was leaving for Maine. "Mr. Montgomery truly has a beautiful collection." Her perfectly made-up face gleamed with avarice. "I'm going to call him with my offer. It's a pity there weren't more ballgowns."

Holly thought of the emerald silk that had prompted daydreams of elegant balls and dancing till dawn.

"Still, you did a fine job, Holly," she said grudgingly.

Holly saw her chance. "Then perhaps we could talk about a raise? The shop's profits are up from last year and—" She faltered under her boss's frown.

"And so are my costs. Holly, you are a wonderful worker and do a beautiful job with the shop in my absence, which is why I give you such a healthy discount on the clothing you buy from me and freedom to work around your children's schedule when necessary. But I don't see how I can afford to give you a raise just now. After all, your settlement from Ron must have been generous.''

Where on earth had her boss gotten the idea she'd received a generous settlement from Ron? And how would clothing for herself, which she seldom splurged on, no matter how good the discount, help her shop for Caroline and Ryan?

''And my costs have also increased, Celia,'' she said gently. ''I really do need a raise.''

''Perhaps in the fall.'' Celia's expression indicated the conversation was over. ''I have several garment bags back there from Mrs. Webb. Fill out the sheets, will you? I'll make a quick check of the receipts and be off.'' She disappeared into the rear of the store.

Holly looked after her boss. If there were any witches in Salem, Celia Parker was certainly one of them.

''I'M POSITIVE OLD Humphrey visited me in my bedroom last night.'' Letitia sat down at the white wrought-iron table across from Jack, who was taking an afternoon break and watching the landscaping crew set the overgrown flower garden to rights. She put her coffee cup on the glass top. ''Jack, are you listening to me? I said I thought I saw a ghost.''

He looked unsympathetic.

''Have a nice dinner with Holly?''

Jack looked at her sharply. She smiled.

''Mrs. Boggs said you called to say you'd be dining out. Since you'd left here with the Bennett children, it was easy enough to guess you probably had dinner with the Bennett children's mother. Did you enjoy yourself?''

Ivy for assistance. Her friend smiled as if to say, *You're on your own.*

"For the past four years I lived in a very old farmhouse, and plumbers or carpenters weren't always readily available. So I did a lot of the work myself. Here, I hire experts because an amateur can easily botch up historic renovations. I know my limitations," he explained. He opened the screen door and walked inside, calling out, "Caro, Ryan, how about some help fixing your mom's sink?"

"The man has limitations?" Ivy sighed. "Funny, I don't see any. He doesn't even need an aura. He's just fine the way he is."

Holly turned on her friend. "*You* were the one who told me he didn't have an aura and therefore wasn't the right man for me. Aunt Prudence and Aunt Patience, however, see a wonderful future for him. Now, what does *that* tell you?"

She shrugged. "Maybe they're right for once."

"Ivy, I have enough trouble keeping my life together. I can't afford complications in the form of a man. Especially a man like Jack." She kept her voice low. Considering everything else he could do, she wouldn't be surprised if he had supernatural hearing powers.

"Why not a man like Jack?"

Holly should have known better. Ivy was like a terrier; once she got her teeth into something, she wouldn't let it go.

Her green eyes grew bleak. "Oh, Ivy, isn't it obvious? Ordinary workaday single mothers aren't usually the stuff of a rich single man's fantasies." Even if he *was* rapidly becoming the stuff of hers.

For a woman who spouted off about not wanting a man in her life, the trouble was, she did. She wanted this man. Too much. The last time she'd wanted a man that way, she'd gotten a little boy. And the boy had run away from home. She didn't think she could endure it if the man left, too.

"Then give me one good reason he's here," Ivy pointed out.

"Because. . ." Holly shut her mouth abruptly.

She smirked. "You can't think of any, can you?" Ivy turned away. "Give it up, Holly. Sit back and enjoy the man while you can." She headed toward her weeding. "As soon as Kevin gets home, I'll send him over to do your mowing."

"Why don't I let him off the hook." Jack walked outside. "The sinks drains a lot better without a dishrag jammed in the garbage disposal," he told Holly.

Holly closed her eyes. "If this was Friday the thirteenth, I could understand all this," she said and sighed.

He eyed the lawn mower dubiously. "No wonder it feels like tough going. Those blades need a good sharpening. Where can I take it?"

"You don't—" Holly's protest was drowned out by Ivy's cheerful intervention with the name of and directions to a local hardware store.

"You can't put that horrible thing in your car!" Holly protested, watching Jack lift the mower.

He cocked his head to one side. "Then it's a good thing I brought my new truck, instead." He smiled. "I'll be back soon."

"Can I come?" Ryan stood on the back porch, hopping from one foot to the other.

"No!" Holly snapped. "You're going to wait for me to come up with a suitable punishment for your clogging up the toilet, playing Indy 500 on the stairs, and quite possibly feeding the garbage disposal a dishrag!"

"Why don't you have him do some weeding?" Jack suggested.

"What a good idea. You heard it, Ryan. Weed." She couldn't resist following Jack down the driveway to watch him hoist the mower into the back of a shiny black truck. "Is there some reason everything you own is black?" she finally dared to ask.

"My mother always said you can't go wrong with basic black. Be back soon." He climbed into the cab.

She remained on the sidewalk as he pulled away from the curb and drove off.

"What's he doing here?" Kevin stopped his bicycle next to Holly.

"I'm not sure," she murmured.

Kevin looked after the departing truck with blatant suspicion. "There's something funny about that guy."

"I don't know if I'd call it funny." Holly turned back toward the house.

"Yeah, then how come there's always strange lights at his house, and his so-called sister looks just like the cat he has? And why does he always wear back, like some kind of vampire?" he questioned. "And how come since he's moved into that house, no one's seen old Humphrey floating around anymore?" He lowered his voice. "That guy isn't human, Holly. And I'm gonna prove it."

"Kevin, you've been listening to some of the more superstitious people in town," she protested. "There's no such things as ghosts. 'Sightings' of Humphrey were probably wisps of fog—or the result of a few too many drinks, that's all."

"Then how come nobody knows what this guy does for a living? They say he's from Europe. Well, Transylvania's in Europe. I know, 'cause I looked it up," he pointed out. "He doesn't talk about himself very much. I bet he doesn't even eat real food."

"Yes, he does," Holly murmured, remembering the prime rib he'd ordered. The very *rare* prime rib. She shook her head violently. "Kevin, I want you to stop these fanciful notions," she said sternly, turning away. Ryan probably wouldn't do any weeding as long as she wasn't there to oversee him. "And I don't want you to say any of this to Caro and Ryan."

"But it's their fault he's even here!" he blurted out.

She halted. "What do you mean, it's their fault?"

"They...they were the ones who went out there that day to see him, right?" he said carefully. He didn't dare bring up his mom's book of spells. He was still relieved it had been returned, and he wasn't about to get into trouble now by opening his big mouth.

Holly walked toward him. "Kevin, if you know something, I'd like to hear it now."

He forced himself to look her squarely in the eye. "All I know is what I've told you."

She wasn't convinced, but Kevin was a master of evasion.

"Don't worry, Holly, I won't let anything happen to you," he vowed.

She sighed. She knew there was no use trying to get a reliable answer from him. "You'd better get home before your mother wonders if you left the country.'' She walked back up the driveway.

Kevin looked over his shoulder in the direction Jack had taken. ''You're not going to put any spells on Holly if I can help it,'' he muttered, thinking of the books he'd found among his mother's collection that should shed some light on the subject of banishing conjured-up beings. As soon as he could, he meant to find the spell that would send Jack Montgomery back to wherever he belonged.

''I SWEAR, THE MAN has turned lawn mowing into an erotic art.''

Holly groaned out loud at her friend's observation. ''You are impossible, Ivy. Maybe *you* need to find a man.''

She lifted her hands, palms upward. ''I did. Trouble is, he's interested in my best friend. Holly, look at the way his muscles ripple as he pushes that blasted mower. It's enough to make you want to jump his bones. Be still, my heart!''

Holly didn't have to look. She already had. And she'd seen a bare-chested man with sweat glistening on his pecs and provocatively dampening the waistband of his cutoffs. ''I wish I knew why he was doing this.''

Ivy slanted a sly glance in her direction. ''Maybe he wants to kidnap and enslave you, and he's conscientious enough to free you of your mundane chores first. How come I can't find someone like that?''

Holly rolled her eyes.

''You know, maybe he's a Scorpio,'' she mused, tapping her forefinger against her chin. ''Everyone knows how intense they are—especially at lovemaking. Perhaps that's why he keeps his aura hidden—to mask that incredible virility of his. One thing's for sure. A vampire wouldn't survive all that sun. Not to mention have that incredible tan."

Holly fanned her face with her hand. Discussing the man's blatant virility wasn't helping her cool off. "Ivy, wipe your chin. You're drooling," she pointed out dryly.

"My social life is in the toilet. Let me have what little vicarious fun I can. Jack!" she called out. "We're going to be barbecuing hamburgers in a little while. Why don't you join us? And ask your sister, too," she added in a polite afterthought.

"Ivy!" Holly hissed, poking her friend in the ribs.

He halted long enough to wipe his arm across his forehead. "Sounds good to me," he called back. His eyes danced with amusement as they discerned Holly's mortification. "I should be finished with this in the next half-hour."

"Fine. Holly and I'll get started on the food, then," Ivy said brightly.

He nodded and returned to his work.

Holly grasped her friend's arm in a punishing grip and steered her into the back yard. "Why did you do that?"

"Because he deserves a special thank-you," she said sweetly. "Besides, it'll give me a chance to study him for mystical powers," she added.

"There is no such thing as magic, Ivy," Holly warned.

Ivy smiled. "Holly, my dear, there's all kinds of magic. Don't scoff at something you haven't experienced yet." She patted her friend's hand and walked off.

Holly watched Ivy return to her yard. The swishing sound of the mower mingled with Ryan's war whoops as he attacked "invader weeds." She did the only thing a sane person could do. She escaped into the house.

IVY INSPECTED HER GARDEN, pleased to see it weed-free again, when a flash of color in a corner of the yard caught her attention. She moved closer to find Caroline sitting cross-legged on the grass under the dubious shade of an overgrown shrub.

"Why, Caro, what are you doing back here?" she asked.

"Thinking."

Ivy sank down on the grass next to her. "It must be pretty serious thinking if you're all the way back here," she probed delicately.

Caro looked up with her mother's serious eyes. "Aunt Ivy, do you believe one of your books could make someone real from a magazine picture?"

She frowned. "Make someone real? Do you mean conjure up a playmate?"

Caro hesitated. "Sort of. You have all those books of magic you said can make people well or make people fall in love and things like that. Do you honestly believe they can do all that?" Her eyes pleaded for a truthful answer.

Ivy stood up and held out her hand. "Let's go inside and get something cold to drink while we talk."

The girl hesitated. "Please don't tell Mom."

She smiled. "Don't worry. This will just be between us. I promise."

Thus assured, Caroline took her honorary aunt's hand, and the two walked through the rear screened porch into the kitchen, where Ivy settled Caro in the breakfast nook while she poured them glasses of icy soda and set out a package of cookies.

"We won't tell Mom about the cookies, either," Ivy said with a conspiratorial smile. She sat down and waited for Caro to speak.

"Jack isn't real. We made him up from one of your books."

"Kevin took my book of Elizabethan spells, didn't he?" she said softly.

Caro hung her head. "He only did it because he wanted to help us," she said in a rush, still refusing to look at Ivy. "We paid him three dollars to help us get a dad. He said the book would conjure up a man Mom could fall in love with, and he'd become our dad."

Ivy sipped her soda. "Why don't you tell me the whole story," she suggested. "Such as where Kevin cast the spell and how?"

Caro took a deep breath and told her story, beginning with the night of summer solstice in Humphrey Williams's meadow, the pictures cut from magazines, depicting what she and Ryan wanted for a father, including the puppies, the chalk circle drawn in the meadow, the mysterious fog and the sudden appearance of Jack Montgomery. Ivy said nothing when Caro related Kevin's flight but privately resolved to come up with an appropriate punishment for his abandoning the younger children. Caro explained that she hadn't wanted to get in Jack's car that night, but he had given them the impression that they could trust him. The trouble was, now people in town were wondering who Jack really was, and his sister, Caro solemnly informed her, was really a cat.

"The cat wears a collar the same color as Letitia's clothing," she explained. "And her fur is the same color as Letitia's hair. And you never see them in the same room together at the same time."

Ivy silently digested all the information. "Tell me, Caro, isn't Jack the kind of man you'd like for a father?"

"Oh, it isn't that," she protested. "He's practically perfect. I just wonder what will happen when the magic spell wears off and he suddenly disappears. How will Mom feel if she falls in love with him and he goes back to wherever he came from? What would I tell her? All Ryan cares about is getting a dad who will let him have a puppy and be there when he gets old enough for Little League."

"What about you? What do you want a dad for?" she asked quietly, casually munching on a cookie.

"I want Mom to be happy. She wants us to believe that Dad loves us, but we know better." There was resignation on the tiny face. "He wants to be with Eileen because she doesn't have any kids and he thinks she's more fun. He doesn't think that Mom's fun anymore, but she is. She plays games with us, and she made sure we got to go to day camp this summer, even though Dad didn't want to pay for it. I may be a kid, but I can understand things. Dad said he never wanted kids, but I think Jack does, and he likes us and we like him. But if he's made from magic, I'll always worry he'll disappear, and Mom will be unhappy again." Her eyes filled with tears. "She doesn't believe in magic, so I can't tell her what we did. I can tell she doesn't know why Jack comes around her, but he likes her. I know he does."

"There's all kinds of magic, Caro," Ivy began slowly, desperately searching for the right words for the troubled little girl. "Some we find in the books I sell, others we make ourselves. Is Jack magic? Maybe, maybe not. Perhaps he happened to be in the right place at the right time, and a special magic brought him here when he was most needed. And maybe he'll find what *he* was unconsciously looking for."

She laughed. "Now I sound like one of those radio psychologists." She looked back at Caroline. "Sweetheart, do yourself a favor. Enjoy your childhood while you have it, and let us adults worry about finding the right man for your mom, okay?" Lightening the mood, she said wryly, "I will admit, though, it wouldn't have hurt that son of mine to conjure up someone like Jack for me."

"Maybe we could do it again," Caro offered.

"No thanks, kid. Knowing Kevin, he'd have cut out a picture from his horror comics for my ideal mate," Ivy said dryly.

"You won't tell Mom, will you?" Caroline pleaded. "She'll be really mad we were out that night, and even madder because of what we did."

"No, I won't tell her," Ivy assured her. "I'm just glad you realize how dangerous it was for you kids to be out there so late at night. I hate to think what could have happened if someone not as nice as Jack had come upon you. I want you to promise me you'll never do anything like that again," she said sternly. "If anything happened to you kids, your mother would be devastated."

Caro's head bobbed up and down. "I learned my lesson, Aunt Ivy," she vowed.

"I'll make sure Kevin returns your three dollars to you," Ivy promised.

"No, we paid him for a spell, and Jack did appear. So I guess he deserves to keep the money. Besides, he's probably spent it already," she said pragmatically.

Ivy burst out laughing at Caro's accurate assessment of her son. "It's thinking like that that sees you married to the guy fifteen years down the road."

Caro's eyes widened in horror. "Me, marry Kevin? Uh-*uh!*"

"Famous last words, Caroline Bennett. Famous last words."

# *Chapter Ten*

"He's not real," Kevin muttered, standing at his bedroom window to look out over the backyard. "Nobody else can get the barbecue to fire up that easily. And he didn't have any trouble with that old mower, either. No one real could do all that." He looked over at Ryan, who, having been released from the dreaded weeding, sat cross-legged in the middle of Kevin's unmade bed, looking through the boy's collection of G. I. Joe comic books. "He must have snapped his fingers or said some spell to make the fire start up so fast and the mower to work."

"You screwed up the spell, and we still want our three dollars back," Ryan insisted.

"I didn't screw it up. If he's not real, *I* was the one who made him up. And even if he is real, he still showed up after I said the spell," he argued. "But if he's not real, I'll prove it."

"How?" The younger boy was skeptical.

"There's ways." Kevin crawled partway under his bed and pulled out another book. "Lots of ways, if you know what to do."

"That's another one of Aunt Ivy's books, isn't it? You're gonna be in a lot of trouble if she knows you've got it."

"She won't know as long as you keep your mouth shut." He carefully opened the book to a page he had marked with a slip of paper. "Now, are you going to help me with this?"

Ryan shook his head. "Uh-uh. You messed this up, you gotta be the one to make it right. And I want that ol' cat changed into a puppy," he ordered, sliding off the bed and running out of the room. "I hate cats!"

"If you want a puppy, it's gonna cost you extra!" Kevin yelled after him before returning to his post at the window, where he watched Jack overseeing the charcoal fire. "Yeah, we'll see just what you are," he muttered.

"THE WAY JACK IS TENDING that fire, you'd think he'd done it millions of times," Letitia laughed as she helped Holly make potato salad.

"I wouldn't think backyard barbecues are common in the capitals of Europe," Holly commented, rummaging through her spices. "Where is that blasted paprika?"

Letitia reached around her, deftly retrieved the correct jar and handed it to her. "Jack makes you uneasy, doesn't he? And you aren't very comfortable around me, either, are you?"

Holly flushed. "I feel like a hick."

Letitia's eyes softened. "We *can* be pretty formidable, I guess. But that hardly makes you a hick. So tell me, do you think you could be seriously attracted to my rogue of a brother?" she asked with the sudden change of subject she was known for. "If so, I'll happily list all his good points—it'll only take a few seconds."

Holly had just taken a sip of iced tea, and the liquid went down wrong. She choked and began coughing so much that a worried Letitia thumped her on the back.

"Are you all right?" she inquired as Holly gasped for breath. She took the glass out of her hand and set it on the counter.

"I was . . . just surprised, that's all," she wheezed.

Letitia braced a hip against the table. "I know, I'm too blunt at times." She sighed. "Jack says I need to temper my tongue, but it isn't easy. I've always felt if you want to know something, you shouldn't be afraid to come right out and ask. So, is my big brother sexy or what?"

Needing to do something, anything, Holly picked up a vegetable peeler and began peeling everything in sight. "I don't think you understand," she said quietly. "I went through a divorce not too long ago, and romance isn't very high on my list right now."

"Your divorce was more than two years ago—Clare's Hair Palace is a very informative place," she added without guilt.

Holly nodded wryly. Salon networking often put the "old boys' executive bathroom" to shame. She soon got serious, though. "Letitia, I have two children to think about, and an ex-husband who couldn't give a damn about any of us. I also live in a town where privacy is nothing more than a word in the dictionary. There's already gossip about Jack and me just because he took the kids out one day and took me to dinner that night. It makes me uncomfortable to have my family under that kind of scrutiny," she murmured, keeping her eyes on her task.

"You still haven't answered my question."

The pause hung heavily in the air. "Yes, I find your brother attractive." The truth was grudgingly given.

Letitia smiled. Holly was attracted to Jack. Jack was attracted to Holly. Now all she had to do was find a way to get the two alone long enough for Jack to storm Holly's defenses.

"Now I'd like to ask you a less personal question. Do you always peel oranges after you've taken off the skins?"

Holly looked down at the pulpy shreds in her hand. "Naturally," she said with dignity. "I use them to decorate my salads."

Letitia glanced at the potato salad now resting in the middle of the table. "Then if you don't mind, I'm taking this one outside before you do something to it you'll later regret." She picked up the bowl and headed for the screen door, smiling her thanks at Ivy, who held it open for her before coming inside.

"If she wasn't so nice, I could hate her," Ivy said fervently, opening the refrigerator door and pulling out the pitcher of iced tea to refill the glass she held. "No one should be able to get away with shorts that brief. I bet she doesn't even know what cellulite is. Do you suppose she's really eighty years old and goes to those Swiss spas that use monkey or sheep glands? Or that perhaps she's had plastic surgery done on her entire body?"

The tension that had built up in Holly during Letitia's gentle yet persistent interrogation lightened. "I don't think that's her style."

"I wonder if Jack has any rich friends who wouldn't mind a woman with dimpled thighs and hair that hasn't seen its natural color since she was fifteen," she mused.

"Ask Jack." Holly seasoned the hamburger meat and began shaping the patties.

"Ask me what?"

Holly refused to be shaken again so soon, even if Jack had sneaked up on her once more. "Ivy would like to know if you have any rich friends who would take her away from all this," she said evenly, concentrating on shaping each patty into a perfect circle.

"Names and bank-account balances would be more than sufficient," Ivy said lightly, sending a wink in Jack's direction. "I'd better get outside and make sure the kids are setting the table and not involved in making each other's lives miserable." The screen door banged loudly behind her.

"I'm glad your sister could come," Holly said.

"It was nice of you two to invite her." He stood close to her side. "Ticia likes you. And she doesn't usually make snap decisions about people."

"I like her. She doesn't mince words."

"Yes, you always know where you stand with her."

She glanced at him out of the corner of her eye. "I'll have the hamburger patties ready in just a minute."

"There's no rush." Completely at ease, he crossed his arms over his chest and smiled. "We never seem to have time to talk."

"I wasn't aware we needed any."

"It's the best way for us to find out each other's hidden traits," he said. "Such as," he continued before she could protest, "what's your favorite kind of books?"

She bit her lower lip. Her choice of reading material used to be a source of great amusement to Ron. Yet she sensed that Jack, who stood so close to her she could feel the heat from his body, wasn't about to let it go until she answered him.

"Come on," he urged. "I'll tell you mine if you tell me yours."

"Romances. Anything that has a happy ending."

He wasn't surprised. For a woman who didn't believe in magic, Holly seemed to hunger for it, anyway. "With me, it's horror. Not the gory, blood-splattering kind," he hastened to add. "The kind of psychological horror that makes you think twice."

Holly shuddered. "Horror is horror," she said candidly. "And all it does is provide nightmares."

Jack silently hoped she wasn't too wedded to that antipathy. Otherwise, she might disappear the moment she found out what he did for a living. "Music?"

"Classical."

"Golden oldies. Sixties and seventies."

While her manner appeared solemn, mischievous laughter danced in her eyes. "It appears, Mr. Montgomery, we don't have much in common."

"Sure we do," he murmured, uncrossing his arms. "There's something called chemistry. Besides, if people have everything in common, there's no challenge. Hey, I'm giving you a chance to learn all about me. So ask away."

"Why do you always wear black?" she asked again.

He looked down at his black polo shirt and black cotton shorts. "I told you. Black's basic, and I'm a basic kind of guy."

"No, really."

"It would be so easy to lose myself in those eyes of yours," he said softly. "They're enough to seduce a man into revealing anything."

"So why the black?" she persisted.

He made a face, then said slowly, "Before I met you, black always seemed appropriate." For a horror writer his image, to be sure. But maybe also for his mood? he wondered now.

"Appropriate for what?"

"For me," he evaded. "It's sort of become my trademark."

"A trademark for what?"

He leaned over until his lips barely touched the delicate curve of her ear. "Isn't black considered a sexy color?" he asked, distracting her from her line of questioning. His breath was warm against her skin.

She felt her own breath constricting. "It depends on the person."

"The person wearing it or the person seeing it?" He angled his body even closer. He edged his forefinger under her tank top strap, rubbing the slightly callused tip back and forth over her skin. Her hair, coming loose from the clip holding it up, brushed against the back of his hand in a light caress as her head tipped ever so slightly to one side.

"Jack..." She had no idea what she was going to say.

Now his head dipped even farther so his lips rested just above her pulse point. His teeth grazed the skin, sending ripples of sensation along her nerve endings. "If it wasn't for the fact that someone could barge in here at any moment, I'd kiss you senseless, Holly Bennett," he whispered against her throat, teasing her rapid pulse with the tip of his tongue. "I'd take you into my arms and kiss you until neither one of us would be able to stop."

Her laughter stuck in her throat. She doubted any man had ever wanted to kiss her so badly that he couldn't stop once he started. But Jack was right about one thing. Once he started, *she* certainly wouldn't want to stop!

"Considering that your dear sister and my best friend are probably out there plotting our so-called romance, no one would be allowed in this house under pain of death. Still, I don't think it would be a good idea."

"I don't think even the threat of a gory end would bother Kevin. He's been watching me like a hawk all afternoon." His teeth lightly nipped her skin, tasting the moisture filming the delicate surface. "I have an idea he doesn't trust me very much."

She smiled. "He doesn't trust very many people," she said breathlessly, turning her face a fraction of an inch.

Her silent invitation was more than enough for Jack. He grasped her shoulders and turned her body the rest of the way as his mouth covered hers in the kind of kiss that Holly had only read about in her books. She decided then and there that the real thing was infinitely more satisfying. This was the kind of kiss a woman felt all the way down to her toes, the kind that left her sizzling with sensual heat. Hearts thudding, pulses pounding, temperature rising—and here she'd thought it only happened in novels. That, and more, sent her senses reeling as Jack's tongue probed the seam of her lips and beyond to sweep through the moist cavern of her mouth.

"Now I know why oranges are my favorite fruit," he whispered, tasting its essence on her tongue. His hands on her hips pressed her against him. "I wanted to do this that day in the meadow," he murmured, "but I was afraid of scaring you off."

She tilted her head back to see his face better. The glow in his dark eyes didn't unnerve her as much as it used to, even as it silently sent new messages to her senses. Since he'd taken a shower when he went home to pick up Letitia, he smelled of the lime-scented soap he'd used. That and the faint hint of sun-warmed skin were suddenly more intoxicating than any bottled scent.

"From the beginning," he said, "I've wondered if you had more freckles than just those on your nose." He traced one of the sun-kissed circles in the area between her nose and lips. "I want the chance to find them and kiss every one."

She wrinkled her nose. "I hate freckles."

"Freckles are sexy. As is this." He kissed the tiny mark by her mouth.

Holly didn't think she could stop smiling. The man was making her downright drunk with desire, and she loved it! "You're making me giddy, Mr. Montgomery, sir."

"I'll see if I can do more than that later." He cocked his head to one side as he heard loud complaints of hunger issue from the backyard. "I'd better get the hamburgers on before they all collapse from starvation." He reached around her and picked up the plate of hamburger patties. "We'll continue this later," he murmured, dropping a light kiss on her lips.

Holly could only lean against the counter, touching her lips with her fingertips, a dreamy smile on her face.

Forcing herself to return to reality, she quickly grabbed the hamburger buns and the pitcher of iced tea, used her hip to bump open the screen door and walked outside.

"Anything else we need?" she called out. Caroline and Ryan were playing tag with Ivy and Letitia.

"Garlic," Kevin mumbled from the sidelines, his eyes glued to Jack.

"Kevin," Holly said as she arranged the plates on Ivy's picnic table, "could you help me out by getting the condiments?"

"Huh?"

"Catsup, relish, mustard and all the other goodies you like to pile on your hamburger."

He narrowed his eyes at Jack's back, as if to say *I'm watching you,* then shrugged and walked off. In record time he was back, laden down with bottles and jars, which he tumbled onto one end of the table.

"Garlic salt?" Holly held up the bottle. She looked at Kevin quizzically as he returned to his post near Jack.

"I'm surprised you got him to leave the yard for more than three seconds." Ivy had brought out a covered cake and now placed it on the other end of the table. "He hasn't taken his eyes off Jack once."

"I've noticed. What I can't understand is why he's so suspicious of Jack," Holly commented, watching Kevin with a worried frown.

"Holly, Kevin is suspicious of everyone. I can see him growing up to be the head of the CIA. How are the hamburgers doing?" Ivy called out to Jack.

"They're just about ready."

"We should have brought some caviar," Letitia said from her curled up position on a lawn chair. Her eyes twinkled with amusement.

"I tried caviar once." Holly winced. "It was too salty."

"It is an acquired taste," Letitia agreed.

"Where did you used to live?" Kevin asked her bluntly.

"In a four-hundred-year-old villa outside Rome," she replied, wrinkling her nose. "No air-conditioning, no central heat and servants who were more snobbish than their employers. We also had a house along one of the Venetian canals. It was just as bad."

A crafty look entered his eyes. "How was it when it was new?"

Letitia arched an eyebrow. "No air-conditioning, no central heat, the peasants revolting against the aristocracy all the time. What do you think?" she asked huskily, waving a languid hand.

Kevin reared back, staring at the long, manicured nails.

"Kevin, she's teasing you." Ivy spoke up, easily guessing the direction of his thoughts.

He didn't look convinced. "Yeah, right."

"Does your villa have ghosts?" Caro asked, wide-eyed.

"My ex-husband is descended from a very old Italian family," Letitia said. "There's always stories about old family ghosts, but I never saw anything out of the ordinary while I lived there."

"You have an ex-husband like Mom does?" Ryan piped up. "Does he live with someone like dumb ol' Eileen?"

Letitia flashed Holly a sympathetic smile before returning her attention to Ryan. "No, sweetheart. My ex-husband prefers polo ponies."

His eyes lit up. "Ponies? They're almost as good as puppies. But—" he hesitated "—I guess you don't like puppies, do you?"

"Why not?"

"Because you're a cat. And cats don't like dogs."

"Ryan!" This time it was Holly who intervened.

"Good going, pea brain," Kevin muttered. "You're going to give it all away."

Letitia laughed. "I've been called catty before, but... What makes you think I'm a cat, Ryan?"

"Because I saw you turn into a cat at your house. And the cat's collar is always the same color as what you're wearing," he explained solemnly. "Do you think you could turn into a puppy? Just for a little while?"

"Hamburgers are ready," Jack announced, oblivious of Letitia and Ryan's unusual conversation.

"Just in time," Ivy muttered.

Letitia swung around to Holly. "What do I say now?" she mouthed.

Holly could only shrug helplessly. "Ryan, why would you believe Letitia was a cat?"

"Kevin said she was."

All eyes turned in the boy's direction.

"No one's ever seen them at the same time," he argued in his own defense. "And how come the cat's fur is the same color as her hair?"

"It took my hairdresser a long time to come up with this color," Letitia said firmly, "and I'm never going back to that horrible brown again."

"I feel as if I'm missing something here." Holly looked from one to the other.

"Let's eat." Jack set the hamburgers on the table. He sent his sister a warning look. Then he placed his hand on Holly's arm to guide her to sit next to him. "I don't know about the rest of you, but I'm starving."

Holly would have liked to see the subject cleared up, but with Jack sitting so close to her that his bare thigh brushed hers, she wasn't sure she really cared.

"How many mirrors do you have in your house?" Kevin asked Jack suddenly.

Jack grinned. "Enough so Ticia knows her makeup is on straight."

"But you don't like them," he persisted.

"Kevin, shut up and eat your hamburger." Ivy's smile was more than a little strained.

"What do you think about silver bullets?"

"Kevin, if you want to celebrate your next birthday, you will quit asking crazy questions and concentrate on your dinner," Ivy suggested. "Then we're all going to the movies."

"But I thought we could watch my video of *The Lost Boys.*" As he pointedly mentioned a movie featuring vampires, his eyes didn't leave Jack's face.

"I don't think so. Ticia and I are taking you kids to a show while Holly and Jack clean up," she explained in the level voice that said, *You will do what Mother says or else.* "And later on, we're going to talk about a book of Elizabethan spells that mysteriously vanished and just as mysteriously reappeared," she said pleasantly.

Kevin wilted.

"Since the two of you are brave enough to take the kids to the show, Holly and I will be only too willing to clean up," Jack said.

For a moment Letitia looked dubious.

"It's only bad if Kevin puts his hands under his armpit to make gross noises," Caroline told her.

"Kevin won't even try it," Ivy warned her son.

Letitia helped herself to potato salad. "Perhaps Ivy can give me the lowdown on the single men in town."

"With your looks and figure, I doubt you'll have any problem." Ivy eyed her with undisguised envy.

"I still remember when she wore braces and was all arms and legs."

Letitia threw a hamburger roll at her brother. "Would you care for me to give away a few of your secrets, big brother?"

"You two will have to come to Holly's birthday party next weekend," Ivy interjected smoothly. "My great-aunts are giving it, and I know they'd love having you."

"Ivy, it might not be something Jack and Letitia would enjoy," Holly protested, blushing hotly.

Jack gazed at her face. "We'd love to come."

"Prudence and Patience are staging the celebration because they consider Holly part of the family, and they love an excuse to party. They also have a beautiful garden they love to show off. And they'll be delighted to tell your fortunes," Ivy said with a chuckle. "Incorrectly, of course."

"A town filled with magic," Jack mused aloud.

"Your kind of town," Letitia murmured.

Kevin looked as if he wanted to leap on that remark but wasn't given a chance.

"There's all kind of magic," Jack said. "Some performed with chants and potions, some performed by the heart."

Ivy silently caught Holly's gaze and lifted her eyebrows. "You have a romantic soul, Jack."

He was looking at Holly. "Only in certain matters."

Holly looked at him, then wished she hadn't. Once ensnared in his deep, dark eyes, she knew she was well and truly lost.

## *Chapter Eleven*

"You didn't have to let Ivy push you into KP duty," Holly said, carrying empty bowls into the house while Jack swept paper plates and plastic utensils into a trash bag before following her into the kitchen. "There isn't all that much to do."

"I think she was playing Cupid." He opened the dishwasher door, took the rinsed bowls out of her hands and placed them inside. "Besides, I have an ulterior motive." He disappeared back outside. Holly heard the sounds of a car door opening and closing. Then he walked back in holding a bottle of wine. "Do you have a corkscrew around?"

She dug it out of a drawer and handed it to him. "I'm afraid my glasses aren't fancy enough for vintage wine."

"It's the company that matters, not the crystal." He grabbed glasses and gently pushed her toward the front of the house. "Why don't we go sit on your porch swing."

Her fingers slipped off the doorknob, and it took two tries to get the door open. When she went to switch on the porch light, he stayed her hand.

"Not tonight."

They sat sipping wine in the dim moonlight and listened to the night sounds: a dog barking in the distance; insects buzzing; muted conversation and laughter from neighboring houses, their windows open to catch the breeze. Jack used the toe of one shoe to keep the swing moving slowly back and forth.

"I like your town, Holly," he said quietly, draping his arm across the back of the swing, his bare skin brushing her shoulders.

She laughed softly. "You must make fast decisions. You haven't lived here very long."

He studied her profile in the moonlight. "I've seen enough to know what I like."

She didn't have to turn her head to know he was looking at her. "Some people would be put off by our more colorful citizens."

"Because Ivy believes in astrology and her great-aunts are psychics? Because the town buzzes with rumors of witchcraft the moment a stranger appears? It's all rather charming in its way."

She cradled her wineglass between her palms. "Ivy's dying to learn your birth time and date so she can work up your chart. If you could somehow produce a visible aura, she'd be extremely happy. She firmly believes they're an important way to learn about a person." She chuckled softly. "She once said if she'd worked up her ex-husband's chart before she married him, she would have run the other way. At least, she hopes she would have had the sense to."

"Ah, but then she wouldn't have Kevin," he added dryly.

Holly's shoulders shook with her laughter. "Kevin is one of a kind. Ivy claims he makes her nuts, but he's also a very loyal kid." Her smile drooped. "When Ron walked out, Kevin came over and told me I wasn't to worry because he would be around to keep us safe. Not too many eleven-year-olds are like that. When a boy in Caro's class maliciously teased her about her father, Kevin gave him a black eye." She winced. "Kevin was given detention for a month, but he never complained. He also told the boy if he ever said anything like that again, next time he'd blacken both eyes."

"I could see Kevin and Caro getting married somewhere down the road," Jack mused, feeling the slide of her body against his every time the swing moved forward.

"Oh, Lord, Kevin as my son-in-law!" Holly's moan was mixed with laughter. "I have enough trouble imagining my baby girl growing up and dating!" More seriously she added, "It's bad enough sometimes when Ryan tries to act like the man of the house when he should be a carefree five-year-old."

"Your marriage wasn't exactly a bed of roses, was it, Holly," Jack said quietly.

She stiffened. "That's right, I forgot that Mrs. Boggs works for you. She knows everything about everyone."

"Holly, she told me out of concern, not out of gossipy malice. She was trying to warn me not to trifle with you, because you'd already been hurt badly and you deserved better." He kept his arm across the back of the swing, his fingers now cupping her shoulder.

She frowned in thought. "Not as badly as I would have been if I'd still loved him," she confessed. "I stopped loving Ron a long time before he left us. I couldn't love or respect a man who didn't give a damn about his own children." She took a healthy sip of wine. "But I'm sure you don't want to hear about that." She laughed. "This wine is very good. After this, I may never be able to stomach the twist-top stuff again."

Jack knew she was deliberately changing the painful subject, and he let her. He fiddled with a lock of her hair, watching the thick strands curl around his fingers. "Your hair seems to glow in the moonlight."

She was relieved he wasn't pressing her further about Ron. "Are you trying to bewitch me with words, Mr. Montgomery?"

"Is it working?" He fingered the feisty red curl.

"I think so."

"Only think so?" He dipped his head so he could nuzzle the back of her neck. "I guess I'd better concentrate more."

Holly's eyes closed, and her lips curved in a smile. "Perhaps you should." She was surprised that she, who was usually so shy, was actually brazenly flirting. It was almost enough to make her believe in magic!

"How about I persuade my sister to baby-sit one evening, and we drive into Boston for dinner and dancing?" His mouth trailed across her throat.

Her heart leaped at the idea of spending an evening in Jack's arms. "No offense, but Letitia doesn't seem exactly the baby-sitter type."

His lips explored her ear. "Blackmail works wonders." He plucked her wineglass out of her hand and set it down beside the swing with his. "Now, let's get serious."

"People might see," Holly feebly protested.

"That's why the porch light is off," he murmured just before his mouth covered hers in a kiss guaranteed to steal her breath away.

Within seconds, Holly could have cared less if the entire population of Salem, past and present, were standing on her front lawn watching them. Jack edged his hand under her top, sliding his palm along her spine in a slow caress.

"Would I find freckles under here?" he whispered against her lips.

"Yes."

All too soon, a coherent conversation was out of the question. His tongue slid along her lips before dipping inside, teasing hers into a sensuous duel. Needing to touch him as well, Holly slipped her hands under Jack's shirt and flattened her palms against his back. Her nipples, pressed tightly against his chest, peaked almost painfully with her arousal. With only a touch of the fingertips, a tilt of the head, a flick of the tongue, Jack had her aching for more. She whimpered, her body twisting with desire, and he pulled her on top of him, his hips cradling hers.

"Great example for my kids."

The sneering words were more effective than an ice-cold shower. Holly would have leaped up, but Jack kept a firm hold on her.

Ron Bennett climbed the steps and advanced on them. "What the hell is this?" he demanded, stopping at the edge of the swing. He took in the wine-glasses on the floor, Holly's rumpled appearance and glazed eyes. Jack looked implacable as he returned the man's heated stare with a cool, studying one of his own.

"Ron, what are you doing here?" Holly asked, surprised her voice could come out sounding so normal.

"This is my house!"

The touch of Jack's fingers against her back was enough to keep Holly's courage up. "This hasn't been your house for two years."

He shifted from one foot to the other. "Yeah, well, I make the payments on this place."

"You haven't made the payments in more than eight months," Holly reminded him.

"I want to see the kids." His gaze swept over them. "Or have you locked them up so you can sit here in the dark letting this guy feel you up?"

Jack stood up with every intention of beating Ron to a bloody pulp, but Holly's hand on his arm stayed him. She jumped to her feet. "Ron, you gave up all rights to this family two years ago when you walked out." Her voice was calm, Jack's presence giving her the courage she needed to stand up to this offensive man. "What I do is no longer any of your concern, just as what you do with Eileen is none of my concern. I would appreciate your never showing up here again without calling first," she added.

A threatening expression darkened his face, and Ron moved closer. Then Jack speared him with his dark gaze, and he stepped back. "Just who the hell are you, mister?"

"Jack Montgomery."

He shifted his feet. "So you're the one who bought the Williams property. What does a filthy-rich guy like you see in Holly?"

She gasped at his cruel remark, and only Jack's arms around her waist soothed her wounded nerves.

Jack's eyes darkened with fury. "Perhaps I see something in Holly that you never bothered to look for." His gaze could have blasted concrete to dust.

Ron opened his mouth to say something, then closed it with an abrupt snap. "Well, if you're going to fool around like that," he blustered, "you'd better make sure *my* kids don't see anything." He spun on his heel and stalked off.

Holly remained in Jack's arms as Ron drove off. "He's been cruel before, but..." She sighed, resting her head against his chest.

"Hey, easy. He just likes the notion that you might be pining away for him. Seeing us together told him you're definitely not missing him," Jack soothed. "I don't think he's the type who appreciates being replaced." He leaned down and picked up her glass, handing it to her and urging her to take a sip.

"I'm just sorry you had to get caught in the fallout," she said.

Jack covered her free hand with his, lacing their fingers together. "Hey, do I look worried? I'm glad I was here. I don't think he'll bother you anymore."

She smiled wanly. "What will you do, Sorcerer Montgomery? Turn Coach Bennett into a toad?" she whispered, taking the initiative by leaning forward and brushing her lips lightly across his.

He wrapped a hand around the back of her neck and held her close.

"Nay, something far more fitting," he murmured against her lips. "He will be turned into the rug we walk on every time we enter the house. And Mrs. Boggs will use an old-fashioned carpet beater on him at least twice a week." His tongue flicked out and caught a drop of wine glistening by Holly's beauty mark.

She shivered at the touch. "Aye, Sorcerer Montgomery, 'tis a fitting punishment you have come up with. 'Twill be impossible for him to forget his sins."

"Then you'll dance with me in the meadow under a full moon to set the spell spinning?" His teeth grazed the side of her throat.

"Aye," she said with a sigh, closing her eyes in pleasure.

"And lie with me on the dew-kissed grass to greet the sun at first light?"

"To cast more magic spells?" she breathed, tipping her head back. At that moment, she wouldn't have cared if he were a vampire preparing to nip her most vulnerable vein.

"Only the ones to do with us." Her wineglass magically disappeared and both his palms skimmed the waistband of her shorts. "The kind of spells I'm talking about are only for us." This time there was no teasing, only the sure and steady motion of his mouth capturing hers in a searing kiss that short-circuited all thought processes. Holly couldn't remember to breathe, much less think, as Jack lowered himself onto the swing and brought her down on top of him in a heated embrace.

Soft murmurs and sighs punctuated the touch of mouths and tongues, the gentle stroking of hands, as they discovered each other. Holly's nipples rose under the rasp of Jack's lightly callused palms. When he started to lift her top to cover them with his mouth, she came to her senses.

"Someone might see us," she said with regret.

He knew he couldn't leave her open to any more embarrassment, not after what she'd just endured from Ron Bennett. He lowered his hands until they rested on her waist, and he breathed deeply to contain the desire coursing through his veins.

Even in the dim light Holly couldn't miss Jack's arousal bulging against his shorts. It made her want him even more, but, sadly, now wasn't the time. "Everyone will be back soon."

"Not if they know what's good for them." He sighed. "All right, we'll sit here like two old folks moaning about how much the world has changed since our day."

"I'd rather hear about you, your past," she said.

"You forget, I don't have a past. I appeared out of thin air," he whispered dramatically.

"Jack..."

"To be honest, my sweet, I don't have a very interesting past," he told her, putting an arm around her shoulders and keeping her close to his side. "The present is proving much more interesting, between living in a haunted house and meeting a gorgeous red-haired sorceress who's completely enchanted me."

Holly remembered all the times Ron had kept things from her, and her finely tuned senses told her Jack was doing the same thing right now. But what?

"Remember when I quizzed you earlier about your likes and dislikes?" he said a bit too casually.

She nodded, feeling wary.

"And you know how you wondered why a man who's lived in Europe most of his life would suddenly return to the States?"

She nodded.

Jack turned his face to rest his chin against her hair. "I write books." Holly couldn't turn her head without bumping his chin or nose, and he held her that way so he could finish what he had to say. "I've always loved reading, always loved words. I guess books were a constant in my life as I grew up, while everything around me was always changing—countries, fathers, you name it. And I guess the constantly changing cast of characters in my life got me interested in people, in what made them tick. And sometimes the way we learn most about human motivation is in extreme situations." He paused, then doubled back on his story for a moment. "Anyway, I wrote my first book about ten years ago. It was turned down by every known and not so well-known publisher. One agent, though, said I should keep trying, that my work showed promise. My next effort didn't sell, either," he explained.

"You must have been very discouraged," she said softly.

"No, by then I was damn mad," he said emphatically. "And I figured I'd show all of them. I learned I worked best late at night, so I sat at my computer till all hours typing as if my life depended on it."

"And you sold a book?" she guessed.

"And I sold a book. A novel about something stalking a publisher who had turned down one too many books from the wrong author. The editor said it scared the hell out of him so much, he couldn't turn it down for fear he'd end up like the editor in the book did. One sale led to another."

She nodded as the pieces began falling into place. The haunted mansion and the money to buy it, Pyewacket International, the "trademark" black clothing, his unusual schedule, and his amusement with the town's speculations about him. It had all fed right into his image. "You write horror novels."

He nodded, knowing she would feel the movement against her cheek. He tightened his arms around her, fearing her reaction to the news.

"And you've obviously written and sold quite a few."

"Eight. Six of them have already been published, but only in Europe. My agent decided it was time to bring them to the States, especially since I'm an American by birth and we've received a lot of fan mail from Americans who've bought my books while they were overseas. I may not be Stephen King or Dean Koontz, but I've made a good living at it, and my business manager got me into some sound investments. Since I would have had to come to the U.S. for a promotional tour, anyway, and since I was ready for a change, I decided to buy property here. I have to admit the history behind the Williams house intrigued me."

"Yes, I can see why." Holly chuckled. "How appropriate for a horror writer to live in a haunted house."

His heart a little lighter at her easy response, he confided, "Ticia swears old Humphrey visits her late at night. I think it's just the mice that snobbish cat of hers refuses to catch."

"And because you've only sold in Europe, few people here would know your name," she said, piecing together the facts.

"Only if they'd happened to buy one of my books overseas," he replied, pressing a light kiss against her hairline. "Does—does any of this bother you?"

"That you write about things that go bump in the night?"

"It bothered my ex-wife so much that she left me," Jack said quietly. "She said she couldn't live with a man so involved with the darkness of the human soul. She never understood that probing that darkness implied a belief in the light as well—she just figured I must be some kind of psychopath."

He snapped himself out of his brooding. "I've been asked to do a book tour when my first book comes out here next month." He winced. "Publicity has never been one of my favorite activities. I always feel like a performing monkey or something."

"I'd say looking like a monkey is about the last thing *you* have to worry about. Once readers get a peek at you on television, they'll flock to buy your books." She suddenly felt sad, because she could see this time of theirs coming to an end. He was obviously a huge success in Europe, no matter how modestly he presented himself, and he would be nothing less over here. And what wildly successful man would want to bother with a single mother of two small children whose idea of fun was a backyard barbecue?

She felt tears brimming in her eyes and was grateful for the concealing darkness. For the first time in forever she had started to feel that she could let a man into her life, and now it was going to be over before it could even begin. More fool she. She silently ordered herself to get a grip.

Jack didn't miss her withdrawal, even though it was emotional rather than physical. "I hate doing these tours, but it's part of my job." He grabbed her shoulders. "Don't back away now, Holly. Not when we've come so far."

She was saved from a reply by the sweep of headlights across the driveway next door, followed by the slamming of car doors and excited voices. "They're back." She eased herself out of his grasp. "Which means I have two little ones to put to bed." She stood up, a false smile pasted on her lips. "Did you all have fun?" she called out.

"It depends on what you define as fun," Ivy called back. "I'll see you in the morning. I'm ready to collapse in bed!"

"Kids throw popcorn in movie theaters and slurp their drinks," Letitia said, walking toward them, a sleepy-looking Ryan in her arms. Caroline skipped beside her. "We won't even discuss what else they do. Still, it was an experience I wouldn't have missed for the world." She climbed the steps. "Kids are great. I think I want one."

"That's a two-person job, Ticia," Jack wryly reminded her, taking Ryan out of her arms. When Holly reached for her son, he said, "I'll take him in for you."

"Not necessarily," Letitia countered her brother's observation. "There are sperm banks."

Jack rolled his eyes.

"What's a sperm bank?" Ryan mumbled against Jack's neck.

"Good going, Ticia," Jack grumbled, walking through the front door Holly opened for him.

"Oops," his sister said. "I'm sorry, Holly. How about I make it up to you by getting Caroline ready for bed? Please?" Letitia pleaded.

"If she doesn't mind, I don't."

Letitia took the girl's hand. "Come on, sweetness. Let's get those hands washed, and you'll be in your nightgown in no time." She let Caroline lead her to the bathroom.

"Which one is Ryan's room?" Jack asked.

Holly led him into the room and pulled back the covers. "It's so warm he can just sleep in his underwear," she said quietly, watching Jack set Ryan down on the edge of the bed and easily pull off his T-shirt and shorts, shoes and socks. Then he gently draped the covers over the now sound asleep boy and straightened up.

"They must have had quite a night," he said, softly. He turned and looked at Holly. "So did we. Are you going to throw it all away, Holly?"

"Jack," she said slowly, "you're going to be on the road soon, meeting all kinds of people. When you get back, you're not likely to still be interested in someone like me, who really doesn't have all that much to offer."

His face darkened. "I suggest you take a good long look in the mirror and think about all the people in this town who call you the next best thing to a saint. And you already know how I feel about you. That isn't going to change. Think about that, Holly. You know where I am when you've come to your senses." With the catlike tread she was already familiar with, he left the room.

Holly stayed in Ryan's room listening to Jack's and Letitia's murmurs as they went downstairs.

"Good night, Holly. Thanks for a wonderful time." Letitia's soft voice traveled up to her. "Tell Ivy I'll be in to see her store in the next couple of days."

The click of the front door closing sounded loud and final in the now silent house.

Holly wandered into her bedroom without bothering to turn on the light. Come to her senses? She was afraid she already had.

# *Chapter Twelve*

"He writes horror novels?" Ivy's voice rose to a high-pitched squeak.

Holly nodded.

Ivy picked up a recent purchase, a book dealing with the Spanish Inquisition, and used her old-fashioned quill pen to record it in her inventory log.

"It appears his books are popular in Europe, and now they're going to publish them over here," Holly elaborated.

Ivy frowned as a thought occurred to her. "I can't imagine that writing horror fiction would have anything to do with the lack of an aura," she mused. "I really must do more research on the subject."

Holly glanced at the antique pendulum clock ticking ominously over Ivy's desk. Ivy adored the bizarre, and her shop was almost as strange as the books she carried. It was great PR, Holly thought, which reminded her again of Jack. Damn. It seemed everything reminded her of Jack. How was she going to go on?

"I'd better get back to the shop."

"After the way Celia turned down your request for a raise, she should feel damn lucky you're there at all," Ivy snarled. "I really do need to find a spell to turn her into something disgusting, like mold."

"If only life was that simple." Holly laughed softly, walking toward the door.

"I RECEIVED A CALL from a Prudence Tutweiler today formally inviting me to your birthday party."

Jack's voice, although somewhat stiff right now, warmed Holly over the phone lines. "Please don't feel obligated to attend," she said equally stiffly. "Jack..."

"What?"

"I...I thought you weren't going to talk to me anymore." She twirled the phone cord around her fingers.

"I guess I lied," he said. "I discovered I can't go without hearing your voice any more than I can go without air."

"Now you sound like a romance writer again."

"That's what you do to me. And as for your birthday party, I wouldn't miss it for the world. I'm curious to know how the Tutweilers got my number, though, since it's unlisted."

She chuckled. "Need you ask? They're psychics. I'm sure coming up with a mere telephone number is nothing for those two," she said merrily.

"Oh, I received your boss's offer in the morning mail."

Holly winced. "How bad was it?"

"Let's just say she'll have to up it if she wants a deal. I don't like being taken advantage of."

"Celia's gone again for a few days. When she returns, I'll pass along your message."

"Don't worry, love. I don't expect you to do my dirty work for me. Just have her call me when she gets back." His voice lowered. "I'll make dinner reservations for us for tonight. Can you get a sitter?"

Her heart warmed under his endearment. "I'll get one."

"Good. Will you have enough time to get ready if I pick you up at seven?"

"More than enough. I'll be ready."

AS SHE STOOD BEFORE her full-length bathroom mirror that evening, Holly struggled to pin up her rebellious hair in a more sophisticated style. After several defeats, she finally gave up and settled for a good brushing.

"Why can't we go with you?" Ryan whined from where he sat on her bed.

"Because this evening is for adults only," she explained for probably the hundredth time. "Sweetheart, you and Caro are going to have fun with Kathy tonight," she assured him. "She's bringing over her Nintendo set and hooking it up so you can play games. And you're going to make popcorn." She hugged him and dropped a kiss on top of his head. "Why don't you go downstairs with Caro while I finish getting ready."

His glum expression didn't leave as he hopped off the bed. "I bet if I ask Jack, he'll let me come."

"Don't you dare! Ryan Joshua Bennett, if you say one word to him, you will lose television privileges for the rest of the year!" she threatened. But he was already conveniently out of earshot.

"Holly, your date's here," Kathy, a vivacious seventeen-year-old, called out breathlessly a few minutes later.

After a quick dab of perfume she hoarded for special occasions, Holly headed for the stairs.

If Jack was sexy in casual clothing, he was devastating in more formal attire. The mere sight of him weakened her knees. And the blazing fires in his eyes told her he was just as fascinated with her.

"You look lovely," he said huskily, not caring that a wide-eyed teenager was avidly listening. He turned to Kathy and handed her a slip of paper. "The number of the restaurant we'll be at," he explained. "Also my home number. My sister will be in all evening if there's an emergency and for some reason you can't get hold of us."

Kathy's head bobbed up and down. "Sure," she breathed, not taking her eyes off him.

He turned back to Holly. "Shall we go?"

She quickly hugged Caro and Ryan and reminded them to behave.

"I still don't know why I can't go!" Ryan's wail of outrage followed them to the car.

"My dating is still pretty new to him," Holly said as Jack helped her into the car.

"Yes, I gathered he was having a problem after he tried to bribe me to take him along." He chuckled. "I told him we'd make it a foursome next time."

Next time. She silently admitted she liked the sound of that. "I want you all to myself this evening," he added.

She liked the sound of that, too. ''Do I get a hint as to where we're going?''

''Candlelight, soft music, a view of the bay.'' He spared her a glance. ''Hint enough?''

Holly looked out the window to hide the smile stretching her lips.

She soon learned that Jack's romantic streak was long and wide and not limited to words. The restaurant was as he promised: candles and fresh flowers on each table, classical music playing softly in the background, a table overlooking the water, and servers who cared for them with both deference and respect for their privacy.

''For someone who's been out of the country a long time, you quickly learn your way around,'' Holly commented.

''I've come to the States on occasion, but every day I'm here now, I'm more grateful I made the decision to move back.''

''So am I,'' she softly admitted. Surely her feelings were already written in her eyes for all to see.

Jack admired the coppery glints in Holly's hair, the way her eyes seemed to glow in the candlelight. For a man who had shunned romantic entanglements since his divorce, he'd certainly fallen hard for this redheaded nymph. If anyone had cast a spell here, it seemed Holly had cast one on him. And, oddly, he didn't mind in the least.

Holly had no idea what she ate that night. They talked endlessly, sharing thoughts and dreams and feelings. She talked about her hopes of someday having her own business, and of being able to give Caroline and Ryan all they deserved.

Jack talked about his writing, a new series of books he wanted to start, the earliest set in the 1600s and graduating to the present. His agent and publisher were already excited with the idea.

"Is that why you chose Salem? Because of our history?" Holly asked.

"You must admit it's a rich one—maritime tales, witchcraft trials, haunted houses even today. I intend to blend them all in two families, intertwining their lives down the generations." He took a sip of wine. "Your own family history is fascinating, Holly. The kind that should be told."

A shadow crossed her face. "Priscilla Drake should be allowed to rest in peace. Like many women of her day, she simply knew the healing properties of various herbs, and people came to her for cures. When one of her medicines didn't work and a patient succumbed to illness, she was immediately accused of witchcraft. The very same people who had benefited from wisewomen's knowledge and acquaintance with healing herbs for years gave in to benighted views and irrational fears." She shook her head. "It was a dark time in American history," she said quietly. "I was always secretly glad the judge who condemned her to die later killed himself. Some think he may even have killed himself to join her in the afterlife. What brutal thanks he gave her just because he felt guilty for loving her."

"I saw a drawing of her in one of the local history books. You look enough like her to be her sister."

She touched the tiny mark by her lips. "Right down to my 'witch's mark.'" She looked up at him. "No, Priscilla and the Mortons and their whole sad story should be left back in those dark ages, where it belongs."

"Priscilla was engaged to marry Stephen Morton when that alderman died, supposedly from her herbal medicine. Stephen immediately believed the worst and was one of the first to denounce her as a witch," he said quietly in acknowledgment.

Holly nodded. "Yes, and if you've done your homework you also know he was heir to a large shipping firm, and he died on the anniversary of Priscilla's death. Some say Priscilla came back to avenge her burning. For after that, no Morton male lived past the age of thirty, and they all died tragically. The line died out during the Civil War."

"And you prefer all that to remain buried?"

"Wouldn't you?" she demanded.

"No," he said honestly. "How societies choose their scapegoats, our desires for revenge, just or unjust, can tell us a great deal about human emotions and the dangers of repressing them. I think Priscilla's story *should* be told, Holly, should be used to illuminate aspects of human behavior, no matter how bizarre."

"Is that why you've been seeing me? To find out more about her?" Holly asked with all the suspicion her own insecurities bred.

His fingers circled her wrist in a gentle but firm grip. "Holly, I'm seeing you because I want to." He looked deeply into her emerald eyes. "If my sister wasn't staying with me, I would take you to my house and make love to you until you could *feel* the truth of that."

His rough whisper was electricity to Holly's nerve endings.

"You have to take your blinders off, Holly, so you'll realize just how desirable a woman you are." He rubbed his fingers over the soft skin of her wrist. "Perhaps I should call Ticia and suggest she find somewhere else to stay for the night?"

Her answering smile instantly lightened his heart, even as she readied her obvious refusal.

"While I'm tempted by your suggestion, I have a seventeen-year-old baby-sitter to consider."

"Well, since you at least admit you're tempted, you won't mind if I continue tempting you, will you?"

"Could I stop you?"

"Not a chance."

Holly felt a fledgling power rise up in her under Jack's ardent gaze. "Then I shouldn't have to bother with an answer, should I?"

All Jack knew was that he wanted to be alone with her. He didn't even want to share her with a waiter any longer. "Do you want dessert or coffee?"

She shook her head.

Jack dispensed with the check in record time, and before Holly knew it she was ensconced in his car and they were speeding away from the restaurant.

"What time does your baby-sitter have to be home?"

She turned her head, gazing at his fierce profile lit by the glowing dashboard. "About midnight, although Kathy's mother won't have a heart attack if she's a bit late. They live only a few doors down from me."

When they reached Salem, Holly noticed that Jack was not taking her home. He drove on until they reached the infamous Williams meadow.

"Since we have a while to go before the witching hour, and it's a beautiful night, I thought of a romp in the meadow," he explained.

"A romp, huh?" With the new daring Jack's presence inspired in her, Holly kicked off her cream-colored pumps and skipped across the grass in her stockinged feet. She raised her arms and spun around, laughing at the delicious sensation of the warm night air caressing her legs, the grass gently prickling her feet.

"Long ago there used to be picnics held here every summer," she told him. "Can't you picture it? Women in picture hats and beautiful dresses, men in their summer whites. Even though people feared the house itself, the meadow felt safe enough during the day, although everyone left before dark." She breathed deeply. "It must have been beautiful then. Tables set out with tiny iced cakes, champagne, fresh fruit, all sorts of delicacies. Croquet and badminton games. What a shame they stopped."

Jack stood a short distance off, his suit jacket discarded in the car, his shirtsleeves rolled up to his elbows, his tie loosened. "You're a romantic, Holly Bennett."

She stopped spinning. "You wanted history."

He took his hands out of his pants' pockets and slowly walked toward her. "That isn't all I want."

Holly took a step backward for every step he took forward until a tree halted her retreat. Jack stopped in front of her, his hands braced against the tree trunk, to prevent her escape.

"No more running away, Holly," he ordered softly. "It's time to face your fate."

She kept her eyes fastened on his finely chiseled features. "And you're my fate?"

"As you're mine."

"Magic."

Her whisper fluttered across his mouth as it covered hers in a deep, fulfilling kiss that threatened whatever sanity she might have had left. He wrapped his arms around her, pressing her closer to the heat of his body.

As always, Jack's kiss left her trembling for more. She looped her arms around his neck and arched her body against him as her tongue entered his mouth in search of his.

"I want all of you, Holly," he breathed in her ear, lightly caressing her waist. "But I want you in a large, soft, comfortable bed, where we can make love as often and as long as we like."

She trembled in his embrace. "I'm a mother with two small children, Jack," she choked. "Affairs—"

"Not an affair," he corrected her, nibbling on her earlobe. "More, much more. You'll see soon enough."

And then she no longer wanted the words. She only wanted to lose herself in his arms as his lips trailed along her collarbone, his teeth nipped at her shoulder, and his tongue laved the pounding pulse in her throat. Holly cried out softly as his hands found her aching breasts and lovingly caressed them through the thin silk of her dress.

"Oh, Jack..." she moaned, closing her eyes against the wondrous onslaught of passion.

He stopped her whimpers of desire with the power of his mouth, and by the time he loosened his hold on her, they were both breathing hard.

"It would probably be a good idea to take you home before..." He trailed off ruefully. He straightened up and took hold of her hand, lacing his fingers between hers.

Coming back to earth, she could do no more than nod regretfully. Trembling with frustrated desire, she let Jack lead her to the car. They drove into town in awed silence.

When he parked in front of her house, she pulled down the lighted mirror clipped to the visor and tried to apply some lipstick. Her hands were still shaking in the aftermath of their kisses.

Jack smiled at her vain attempt to mask her slightly swollen lips. There was no hiding the fact that Holly Bennett had been well and thoroughly kissed.

Kathy looked up with a smile of greeting when they walked inside. Jack insisted on paying her, then offered to walk her home, claiming it was no trouble, since Holly would be making coffee for him. His blatant announcement that he wasn't about to leave right away worked. By the time he returned from seeing Kathy to her door, the aroma of fresh-brewed coffee wafted throughout the downstairs.

"To give the gossips something to talk about, I will drink a cup of coffee," he told her, resting his hands on her shoulders. "Then, to frustrate and confuse them, I will give you a very polite kiss at the front door before I drive home. Unfortunately, I have to take an early-morning flight to New York—it's about a talk show appearance.'' His pained expression told her he wasn't happy about it. ''I'll have to be there for a few days, so I probably won't see you until your party.'' He leaned against the kitchen counter, watching her while she filled two cups with coffee. He accepted one and sipped the hot brew.

''You might not find Aunt Prudence and Aunt Patience's parties exactly your cup of tea,'' she warned him again.

''I will as long as you're there.'' He finished his coffee and set the cup down. ''Now come over here so I can kiss you the way I want to before you walk me to the porch, where I'll give you your 'public' kiss.''

After Jack left, Holly could easily tell the difference between Jack's private and public kisses. She liked the private ones much better, she decided, lost in a sensual haze.

There would be no need for a bubble bath, a romantic novel and waltzes playing in the background tonight. Holly knew she had the real thing.

JACK WAS SETTLED on the early-morning commuter flight to Kennedy Airport when it hit him like a ton of bricks: he was in love with Holly Bennett. He stared blankly at the magazine lying open in his lap, but all he could see was her face. Images floated through his mind: Holly naked in his bed, smiling up at him, her emerald eyes glazed from making love all night. Holly laughing and playing with Caroline and Ryan on his front lawn, while Ryan's long-awaited puppy yapped and ran with them. Even more important, Holly, swollen with his child, looking so beautiful he ached.

Could it have been Kevin's spell that had brought them together, after all? he wondered.

"Magic," he murmured.

## *Chapter Thirteen*

"I've heard he keeps a coffin in the basement."

"Really? Laura told me he holds séances every night, and he's been able to contact Humphrey, who told him where he'd hidden a fortune in his wife's jewelry."

"Nonsense, the man bought the house because it's centered in a magnetic field that gives off powerful vibrations. Staying there, he'll live forever."

"You can't tell me that woman is his sister. It's been said a cat with the same color fur as her hair and collars the same color as her clothing prowls the property all night, and no self-respecting dog dares enter. Mind you, the two are never seen at the same time."

"Joe Perry was out there to do an estimate for a swimming pool. I bet it will have black tile."

"He has a dark intensity about him that's downright scary." The woman shuddered but smiled broadly. "And downright thrilling."

"No, I think it's more a lean and hungry look. Entirely appropriate for a vampire."

"Well, honey, he can bite my neck anytime!"

Confidences flew fast and furious as Holly, with a bright smile pasted on her face, circulated among the people milling across the Tutweilers' back lawn.

"Yes, well, he is very good-looking, and sexy in a devilish way," another woman giggled. "My, my, I chose the appropriate description, didn't I?"

"Do you think he turns into a werewolf during a full moon?"

"As far as I'm concerned, he can be a wolf around me anytime!"

"I heard he's lived all over Europe. Maybe he's a secret agent."

"Nah, secret agents are only sexy in the movies. It has to be something a lot darker than that. And he hired Mrs. Boggs, who everyone knows is a witch."

"Can you believe some of these people?" Ivy sidled up to Holly and whispered in her ear.

"I can't believe one man could generate so much speculation," Holly said, holding her punch cup in a white-knuckled grip. "You'd think new people had never moved here before."

"No one like Jack. Hello, Marilyn, how are you?" Ivy nodded and smiled at a friend who passed by. "I can't wait until he shows up. You're going to see women drooling like crazy." She fingered the amethyst crystal she wore on an antique silver chain. "Poor Holly. You must have really missed him these past few days."

She had. Though Jack had telephoned nightly, hearing his voice had only left her aching for the man himself. It warmed her that he always asked about Caroline and Ryan and even talked to each of them one evening when he had been able to call early enough.

"He said his plane was arriving at Logan this morning, and he and Letitia would be here," she said softly.

"Honey, if you don't want people to guess you've fallen in love with the man, you'd better dampen that glow on your face," Ivy advised in a low voice.

Holly whipped her head around. "Excuse me?"

"You heard me." She patted her arm. "And it couldn't happen to a better person." She smiled imp-ishly. "You could almost call it magical. After all, look at the way things have picked up. Celia suddenly caved in and gave you a raise. Your car doesn't have to be kicked and sworn at to start up. And Ron's last support check not only arrived on time, it didn't bounce."

"There's our birthday girl!" Patience wrapped Holly in a lilac-scented hug. It had to be Patience. Prudence preferred attar of roses. "My dear, you look lovely today." The spritely lady looked around. "And where's your young man? Don't tell me his train is late?" She looked upset. "I told Pru he should fly back from Washington instead of taking the train."

"I'm afraid I didn't check the train schedule, Aunt Patience." Holly went along with the pretense rather than try to explain Jack was flying back—from New York. Years of experience had taught her it was much simpler.

"Well, as long as he's here in time to see you cut your cake," she said, beaming. "We baked your fa-vorite—a four-layer coconut cake. I feel this year's our best yet." She hugged Holly again and went off to greet several newcomers.

"I hate coconut cake," Holly said in a small voice, watching the elderly woman laugh at something a friend said.

"You should complain. I get your chocolate fudge cake on my birthday," Ivy teased.

"They are so dear that I don't have the heart to tell them," she explained.

"Don't worry. Just slip me your piece as always," Ivy advised, moving away. "Come on, birthday girl, make nice with your guests."

Holly checked on Caroline and Ryan, who were playing games with the other children in the large sunroom under the supervision of two teenage girls. Once assured they were all right, she wandered back outside.

"If this is a birthday cake, what do they do for major holidays?" a husky voice murmured in her ear.

She spun around so fast, some of her punch spilled over the sides of the cup. Jack plucked the cup out of her hand and set it on a nearby table. The broad grin on his face and the devilish lights in his eyes left her weak-kneed.

"Does this mean you're happy to see me?" he bantered.

She clawed for composure. "You're fishing, Mr. Montgomery. You startled me, that's all. Aunt Patience will be glad your train from Washington wasn't late, after all." Jack arched an eyebrow in question. "She wished she'd advised you to fly."

"Yes, the train from Washington did seem to lag a bit," he said, tongue-in-cheek.

"Happy birthday!" Letitia appeared and enveloped Holly in a Joy-scented hug. "You should have been in New York with us, Holly."

"She wanted company while she shopped," Jack said dryly. "UPS is going to love us for the next week while all her purchases are delivered."

Letitia shot him a look. "Who was the one to practically buy out F.A.O. Schwarz?"

Holly's eyes widened at the name of the famous toy store.

"I bought a couple of things for the kids," he explained.

"A couple?" Letitia turned to Holly. "Caro and Ryan are going to think Christmas came ahead of time."

"Holly, I didn't go overboard," he rushed to assure her. "I just found some things I thought they'd like. You can look everything over before I give it to them to make sure it's appropriate."

Her old reaction would have been instant refusal to accept any extravagant gifts. "I'm sure you wouldn't choose anything wrong for them," she said softly. "Now, perhaps the two of you would like to meet some of your neighbors. Believe me, they're dying to meet you."

Letitia cast a sharp eye around, easily noting the open looks of curiosity from the guests seated at tables or standing around in small clusters. "Yes, and I'd say a majority of them are females interested in meeting Jack."

"You're also a source of conversation," Holly told her. "No one has seen you and your cat at the same time, so they're wondering if you're one and the same."

Letitia threw back her head and laughed. "This is priceless. I must ask Ivy the words to some spells, just so I can keep up appearances." She patted Jack's shoulder. "I'm off to make new friends. You do the same, big brother. All too soon those interviews will be on television, and people will know you for who you *really* are," she teased.

"When Ticia was born I told Mom to send her back, but she didn't listen to me." He heaved a long-suffering sigh. "Ah, well," he added more seriously, "Ticia acts like a spoiled brat sometimes, but she's really a warm and caring person. That someone would betray her trust the way her ex-husband did took a lot out of her."

"There you are, young man." Prudence Tutweiler sailed upon them, engulfing them in the scent of roses. "Holly has been watching for you ever since she arrived. Patience claimed your train would be late, but I told her time and time again you should have driven up from Washington." She rolled her eyes while her hands fluttered dramatically. "She has to learn to focus her energy more to get the vibrations correctly. Holly, we'll cut the cake in about a half hour, so don't disappear." Her bright eyes twinkled as she gazed first at Holly, then at Jack.

"They say big cities are all alike, so perhaps I was in Washington instead of New York," he murmured, clearly dazed by Prudence's unique form of logic.

"That's all right. They baked me a coconut cake, just as they have for the past fifteen years. The thing is, I hate coconut. That's Ivy's favorite, and she gets my chocolate cake on her birthday."

Jack looked around at the lavish trappings for the party: gaily decorated tables, with fresh-flower centerpieces on each, music playing in the background, a buffet table set up under a striped tent.

"They've thrown quite a party," he commented. "They must love you very much."

"I've been an adopted great-niece ever since I can remember," Holly said. "They enjoy using their money to make people happy. They have a ballroom straight out of *The Great Gatsby,* and every year they hold their Halloween costume ball, complete with an orchestra and endless magnums of champagne. Ivy and I couldn't wait until we were old enough to attend."

She looped her arm through his, and they began to walk among the tables. "I'll warn you now, a lot of people are eager to meet you, but so far it's a toss-up whether you have a coffin in the basement or you turn into a werewolf during the full moon."

He chuckled. Then his eyes darkened as he looked down at her. "I missed you these past few days."

Her face glowed under his intense regard. "I missed you, too," she whispered. A woman approached them. "It appears, Mr. Montgomery, you're about to be mobbed."

He ran his fingertips over her wrist. "One woman does not make a mob."

"It only takes one to start. Once she's made contact, the others will follow immediately."

Holly's prediction was correct. One introduction led to another, which led to another and another until at least six women surrounded Jack, who looked more claustrophobic by the moment. Holly smiled and withdrew to the outskirts of the crowd.

"Very cruel, Holly." Letitia appeared at her side and giggled. "Jack hates this kind of attention."

She smiled. Jack might have been surrounded by women, but over their heads he kept flashing secret smiles meant only for her. "They want to know if he sleeps in a coffin."

Letitia looked at the people milling about, most of them covertly watching Jack and whispering among themselves. "Perhaps I should warn you that when I stopped by the sunroom, Ryan was chatting up Jimmy Myers, whose dog just had four puppies."

Holly groaned. "The Myers's dog is half St. Bernard. But it would never occur to Ryan that a tiny puppy could grow into the size of a small horse."

Letitia wiggled her fingers in a gay wave at her brother's scowling face. "Don't let Jack get away, Holly. Something tells me you're the best thing that's ever happened to him." She sighed. "I think I'll see if Ivy has a book on spells that will prove as lucky for me." That said, she walked off looking for Ivy.

A confused frown covered Holly's face as she watched Letitia cross the lawn. "A book of spells?" *Ivy's missing volume of Elizabethan love spells. Magazines with pictures cut out. The book mysteriously reappearing. Jack acting as if he already knew her from the very beginning. Caro and Ryan going to Jack's house, as if they somehow knew him already. And lately, Ivy acting as if she knew something Holly didn't.* The air seemed to grow very thin around her.

Holly spun around to look at Jack. He smiled and winked at her.

"Everyone, we're going to cut the cake now!" Prudence called out. "Gather around."

Forced to back-burner the thoughts threatening to drive her crazy, Holly walked toward the table with the enormous birthday cake.

"We welcome all of you here to celebrate Holly's birthday," Prudence announced to the group, "and we hope you're all enjoying yourselves. We'd also like to welcome two newcomers to our community—Jack Montgomery and his lovely sister Letitia Danova. And now, a toast to Holly." She held up a glass of champagne. "May all her wishes come true."

"I hope she's wishing for a puppy." Ryan's voice rang out, leaving everyone laughing as Holly cut the first piece.

"Too bad you don't like coconut. The ladies make a mean coconut cake," Jack told Holly as she sat at a table with Caro and Ryan, Letitia and Ivy.

She wrinkled her nose as she took a tiny bite.

"If they ever get a prediction right, the whole town would probably have a parade," Ivy said, eating her piece with great relish.

"Everyone is so friendly here," Letitia commented.

"Did Sally Adams really ask you if your dress came in a size six?" Ivy asked. "I don't think that woman was a size six when she was age six!"

Letitia nodded. "I'm not usually so crass, but when I told her that it's a one-of-a-kind design and what I paid for it, she decided the style wasn't for her, after all."

"Sally, of all people, deserves crassness," Ivy declared. "We must go out man-hunting together, Letitia," she decided.

"And here I was hoping to talk them into taking the kids so we could have some time alone," Jack murmured in Holly's ear.

The idea of spending time alone with Jack set her tingling with anticipation. "I could try to bribe Ivy."

He used his fork to snatch a bite of cake off her plate. "And if that doesn't work, I can always threaten Ticia."

"When do you open your presents?" Ryan demanded in a loud voice, bouncing up and down in his seat.

"The guests don't bring presents, Ryan," Holly explained, placing her hand on his arm to calm him down. "This is just a celebration."

"But Aunt Ivy gave you a present."

Her face burned. "That was different. And your Aunt Ivy and I will have a discussion about that later."

Jack's curiosity was piqued. "This sounds interesting. What did she give you?"

"Nothing important," Holly bit out, glaring at her friend.

Ivy was unperturbed. "It was a quaint little statue I found at an auction. The moment I saw it, I knew it was meant for Holly."

"What's it a statue of?" Letitia asked, easily catching on that there was something Holly didn't want Jack to know.

Ivy ignored Holly's warning glare. "Oh, it's a lovely fertility goddess."

Holly blushed eighteen shades of red.

"Sounds like the kind of gift that could come in handy at the right time," Jack murmured, hiding his smile.

"I'm sure Ivy will think so when she gets it back on her birthday."

"She didn't appreciate last year's gift, either." Ivy heaved a melodramatic sigh. "And I'd ordered it specially from Frederick's of Hollywood. It was deliciously *X*-rated."

"What's *X*-rated?" Ryan piped up.

"Something for girls only," Jack said smoothly.

The boy wrinkled his nose in disgust. "Yuck!"

Holly felt as if she was at one of the Mad Hatter's tea parties—and Jack fit in perfectly! She muttered a curse under her breath.

"Not exactly a good example for the children," Jack chided, draping an arm around her shoulders. He brushed a kiss by her temple. "Mmm. I can't wait to get you alone later."

She shook her head ruefully. "The kids aren't exactly at their best after one of these parties. It's going to take me hours to calm them down and get them into bed. By then I'm usually a wreck."

"The shop is closed tomorrow, right?"

She nodded.

"Then why don't you bring them out to the house for lunch?"

She tipped her head back to look at him. "Are you sure?"

"Very."

"Then I accept."

"I'll give you your birthday gift then."

Her lips twitched. "An even better reason to accept."

His fingers traced a random pattern along her bare arm. "Come around twelve."

She glanced at her watch and saw that the afternoon was almost gone. She looked around for her children, who had disappeared. "Naturally, they've probably sensed it's time to leave, and they're going to make it difficult."

Holly smiled when she saw Patience approach. She threw her arms around the older woman. "This has been the best birthday yet," she told her. "But the kids have been running wild all day, and it's going to take me forever to get them back to normal. So we'd best be off."

"And perhaps you'll have some time alone with your young man." Patience sent her a knowing look, then glanced over at Jack, who had once again been corralled by a cluster of partygoers.

"Tonight, I just want some peace and quiet to savor my day," she declared. "But thank you so much for always being there."

Patience kissed her on the cheek. "Then escape while you can. If you're looking for Caroline and Ryan, they're in the kitchen."

"As if they could still be hungry after all they've eaten today," Holly said dryly, heading toward the house.

Holly stopped to thank Prudence, then gathered up Caroline and Ryan and herded them out to her car. Letitia called out to her as they crossed the lawn.

"You're not leaving here without your present from me," she announced, heading for Jack's car. "Wait right there.'' She returned with a gift-wrapped box. ''It's just a little treat,'' she explained.

''You didn't have to do this,'' Holly protested weakly.

''I know, but Jack will tell you I enjoy shopping for others even more than I do for myself.'' Her smile was warm. ''Happy birthday. Enjoy your goodies.'' She kissed her on the cheek.

By then Jack had joined them, and he, too, gave Holly a decorous peck, though his eyes conveyed just how unsatisfying that was. ''May all your fantasies come true, Holly,'' he whispered for her ears only.

''Mom!'' Ryan prompted her, tapping on the car window.

She snapped back to reality. ''Yes, yes, we're going.'' And in a flurry of well-wishes, they were off.

Holly wasn't sure who to thank that the children got ready for bed without too much of an argument. She decided it was a birthday present from them, along with the dusting powder they had presented her with that morning, courtesy, she suspected, of Ivy's guidance.

While her bath water ran, Holly carefully loosened the wrappings on Letitia's gift and slid them off the box.

''Oh, my,'' she whispered. In the package was a book with the kind of cover designed to give one nightmares. But Holly's heart was warmed instead of chilled, for Jack was the author. Beneath the book was a sheer nightgown in a beguiling shade of peach. She fingered the delicate fabric thoughtfully.

''Letitia, you're trying to tell me something, aren't you?'' she murmured.

THE MUSIC WAS STRAUSS, the lighting soft. Holly looked around but could see little beyond the circle of candlelight in which she stood. She had no idea where she was or how she had gotten there. When she looked down, she found she was wearing the emerald-green ballgown she'd seen in Jack's attic. Her rebellious curls were piled on top of her head in an intricate style, and a silk mask covered the top part of her face.

Something prompted her to turn, and she saw a tall figure standing in the shadows a short distance away. When he stepped out of the darkness, she saw that he was dressed in formal black evening attire, with a cutaway jacket and tails. The snowy folds of his shirt highlighted dark features partially hidden by a black silk half mask that effectively shielded his identity. He walked toward her, his hand outstretched. She didn't hesitate to place her hand in his, and he gracefully swung her into the waltz an unseen orchestra played.

"Who are you?" she asked in a hushed whisper.

He smiled. "I am your fantasy, madam." He spoke not another word but silently paid court to her as they danced the dreamlike night away.

Finally, her dance partner smiled, lifted her hand and turned it to press his lips against the delicate skin of her inner wrist. Holly gasped—and sat straight up in bed.

She looked around wildly, but she was in her bedroom, the pale gray dawn peeking through the curtains.

Her wrist tingled unaccountably, and she swung her legs out from under the covers. As she stood up, she felt her feet tingle, too, as if she'd been dancing for hours.

She pressed her fingertips to her brow and glanced up at her reflection in the mirror. Her face showed the glow of a woman who'd just spent an incredibly romantic evening with a mysterious and devilishly handsome man.

Her lips barely moved. "It was a dream.... Wasn't it?"

## *Chapter Fourteen*

"Mom, you're gonna let us go with Aunt Ivy, aren't you?" Ryan hopped from one foot to the other.

Holly looked at her children, then turned to the instigator of this tug-of-war. Ivy smiled blandly.

"We're supposed to go to Jack's house for lunch today," Holly reminded the children.

"They can do that anytime. Let them come with me, Holly," she urged. "It's only overnight. I know this is sudden, but the man just called me last night. He's very eager for that book of obscure Celtic spells I picked up several months ago, and he insists on paying me to drive up to Vermont to deliver it personally. Kevin's going on an overnight with a friend, so I thought I could take your munchkins for chaperons. Besides—" she lowered her voice "—this will give you some time with Jack. Judging from the hot looks passing between the two of you at the party yesterday, you need it."

At Holly's look of outrage, Ivy laughed. "The air was practically sizzling! Seriously, though, you'd be doing me a favor by letting me borrow the kids. I know of this Terence Blake, and he's definitely on the up-and-up, but I'd love some company for the trip. I've heard Blake is absolutely gorgeous," she confided. "If I'm there with the kids, at least I won't make a fool of myself. Please, Holly, do this for me?"

Holly looked at the three pleading faces. She crouched down in front of the two children. "Do you promise to do everything Aunt Ivy says and not give her any trouble?"

Ryan's head bobbed up and down. "I won't even ask her to stop all the time when I need to go to the bathroom."

Ivy laughed. "That's one request I won't complain about."

"Let me pack up a few things for them." Holly headed upstairs.

With a broad smile on her face, Ivy watched her leave. "You did a great job, kids," she said in a low voice.

"You really think us going away will make Mom fall in love with Mr. Montgomery?" Ryan questioned. "I mean, we're only going to be gone overnight."

"It will nudge her in the right direction." Sometimes it only takes one night, she thought, crossing her fingers.

"And this man we're going to see really has puppies?"

"Yes."

Ryan jumped up and down. "Then I think this is a great idea."

"Puppies again," Caro groaned.

Ten minutes later, Holly stood watching Ivy back down the driveway with Ryan and Caroline buckled into the front seat of her station wagon. Just before

Ivy reached the street, she leaned out the open window.

"Oh, I forgot to tell you. Letitia is going along with us, so enjoy your day with Jack!"

Holly's eyes grew wide as saucers. "What? Ivy!" She stamped her foot. "Wait! You don't need the kids." It was too late. The car was already halfway down the street. "Oooh! Just wait until you get home, Ivy Elliott! I'm going to find a spell to turn you into a toad!"

Holly was in a nervous dither as she prepared for her lunch date with Jack. By the time she was ready to leave, a pile of clothing littered her bed, and she was tempted to change yet again. But she was running out of clothes and time.

For once it didn't thrill her that her car started up without a fuss. "There is nothing wrong with my being at his house alone with him," she told herself as she drove. "I'm an adult. He's an adult."

A very *male* adult. A male who's talked about making love to you. A man who's lived in France, where lovemaking is practically an institution. She took a hand off the steering wheel and wiped her damp palm on her car seat.

The house loomed huge before her, imposing even in the daytime, but Holly wasn't frightened of the house. It was the owner who sent shivers down her spine. Then a reassuring thought occurred to her. Mrs. Boggs would be at the mansion!

But it was Jack who opened the door, a broad smile on his face. "The kids told me about their trip when Ivy stopped by to pick up Ticia," he explained, escorting her inside and down the hallway to the French doors that led to the garden.

"Yes, they're looking forward to it. I just hope Letitia can handle all those hours in a car with the children. Trips tend to bring out the worst in them."

They walked outside, and he gestured her to be seated at a glass-topped, wrought-iron table. He poured wine into two glasses and handed her one.

"She'll survive," he said wryly. "All in a good cause. It appears she and Ivy feel we need to be alone, and they'll go to any lengths to promote it."

Holly choked on her wine.

"Are you all right?" He stood behind her to thump her on the back.

"Yes," she wheezed.

"You're not nervous about spending the afternoon alone with me, are you?" he guessed accurately, lowering his head to lightly nibble on her exposed nape.

"But we're not alone. Mrs. Boggs is here."

"It's her day off."

"It—it is?"

"That's right. We're here alone. Scared?"

She strove for a semblance of calm and failed miserably as she squeaked, "No." *Yes.*

He nibbled along the base of her neck. "What if I said the hell with lunch and swept you up into my arms and carried you upstairs to my coffin, where we could while away the rest of the day making mad, passionate love?"

It was growing more and more difficult to think coherently. "Vampires don't have any powers during the day." Her skin tingled from his moist caress.

"This vampire has special powers." He tickled the sensitive spot just behind her ear with the tip of his tongue. "But I suppose we must have food to keep up our strength," he announced. "You sit here and enjoy the view. I'll bring out the food." He disappeared between the French doors before Holly could utter a word.

Enjoy the view? Holly sat there completely unnerved.

Within moments, Jack reappeared, pushing a serving cart in front of him.

"I had Mrs. Boggs prepare something special for us," he explained, maneuvering the cart next to the table. "Dessert is in the refrigerator, and it looks dangerous. Double-chocolate cheesecake."

She allowed him to spoon a little bit of everything onto her plate, still nervous but feeling oddly pampered.

"Now, tell me how you spent the rest of your birthday evening, from which I was so summarily excluded."

Birthday. Fantasy. Dream. She nearly choked again. *Had* he been excluded—or not? she wondered desperately.

"Letitia gave me one of your books. I looked through it last night," she hedged. "*Dark Moon.*"

He looked wary. "And?"

"I'm not sure I'll ever look at moonless nights the same way again. But I liked it. It made me stop and think." She toyed with her lobster salad. "Your ex-wife should have loved the man who wrote the books instead of fearing him."

She looked up, suddenly anxious, and asked, "Was she pretty?"

"She was a photojournalist."

"That's not what I asked. Was she pretty?"

"A lot of people told her she should be on the other end of the camera," he admitted blandly.

Holly put her fork down. She suddenly didn't feel very hungry.

He reached over and clasped her hand. "Holly, don't. Don't run away, don't withdraw again. You're worrying about something in the distant past that isn't important anymore. Stay here in the moment, here with me," he urged with all his dark intensity.

She looked up into his deep brown eyes and read the sincerity there. Just then Le Chat crossed the patio and settled himself on a cushioned chair in a languid pose reminiscent of his mistress. Her heart lighter, Holly said, "Speaking of your dark and distant past, that cat certainly helped your mysterious image along."

Jack matched her light tone with visible relief. "Stupid feline won't even catch mice. He considers himself above such things," he grumbled. "Ticia stayed in New York the entire time that fleabag was in quarantine. Claimed she couldn't let her darling spend all that time without moral support." He shot the cat a look. "The only positive note about him is that he wouldn't dream of shedding on the furniture. It's beneath his dignity."

Holly watched the cat lift one paw and gracefully clean each pad. "I don't think I've ever seen a cat with that color fur before."

"A woman not far from Ticia's ex-husband's villa breeds them." He poured more wine into her glass.

"With all of us divorced, do you ever wonder what's wrong with us?" Holly mused, sipping her wine.

"There's nothing wrong with us. We can't control the bad behavior of others," he corrected her. "Ticia's ex, for example, believed in nonstop parties after his polo matches, and when she found him in bed with three of her so-called good friends, it was the last straw. The sad part is, she really loved him. My ex married me but wanted me to be someone else, someone I wasn't. And yours obviously wanted to have his cake and eat it, too, and his family's feelings or needs be damned."

Holly nodded thoughtfully. "And Ivy's husband thought life revolved around ESPN and any sports event that happened to be on in between poker games, no matter what his wife or son wanted. He drank and gambled and hardly gave his family the time of day. It was tough on both Ivy and Kevin. But they're troupers. Despite their idiosyncrasies, they'll be okay. But what a price they've had to pay."

"Considering Kevin, I would have thought his dad was an international spy." Jack chuckled.

"He owned a garage in town." She sat back. "I couldn't eat another bite."

"Not even Mrs. Boggs's cheesecake?" he tempted.

She shook her head. "I couldn't possibly.

Jack stood up. "Then I'll clear the table while you sit out here and relax."

She started to rise. "I'll help."

He grasped her wrist. "No, this is your day off. I want you to take one of those lounge chairs, lie down and close your eyes." He paused long enough to drop a light kiss on her lips, then efficiently stacked everything on the serving cart and pushed it back into the house.

Again, that unfamiliar sensation of being courted, pampered. Holly smiled on her way over to the nearest chaise longue and collapsed, boneless, on the thick cushion.

Feeling someone staring at her, she opened one eye and found Le Chat seated on the edge of the cushion, watching her with feline curiosity.

"How anyone could mistake you for Letitia is beyond me," she informed the cat, who promptly climbed down the chair and sauntered back into the house.

Given her peculiarly strenuous night and the warmth of the summer day, it didn't take much for Holly to fall into a light doze.

When Jack returned he found her lying on the chaise longue. He leaned over and brushed his lips across hers. She stirred and opened her eyes.

"I'm sorry. I guess I didn't sleep very well last night." Her voice was husky.

He picked up her hand and laced his fingers through hers. "I hope my writing isn't what kept you up."

She smiled. A secret smile. "Not your writing." *You,* she thought. "My life hasn't been very calm since you entered it, Mr. Montgomery. You've managed to quite nicely turn it upside down."

"Is that a complaint?"

She cupped his cheek with her palm. "More like wonderment—that you chose me," she said softly.

He turned his face so that he could gently bite the fleshy part of her palm. "An easy-enough explanation. I met a green-eyed redhead who knocked my socks off. That day in the attic, I seriously thought of closing the door and locking us away for the next twenty years."

Her lashes drooped to hide the expression in her eyes. "That day in your attic, I thought you might do just that."

He wrapped his hand around her wrist to keep her fingers against his cheek. "You wouldn't have protested?"

"I was so nervous that day, I probably wouldn't have had the courage to protest." She shifted to give him more room to sit. "I was trying so hard to act the part of the professional businesswoman."

"I was picturing you in that green ballgown."

Her hand stilled. The green ballgown. The same one she'd worn in her dream.

His smile sent shafts of warmth into her. "We'd dance till dawn." All the time he spoke, his face lowered until it hovered a breath away from hers. "And then I'd whisk you away to ravish you until you were mine, body and soul."

Excitement raced through her veins at his words.

He stared into her eyes as if looking for an answer in their emerald depths.

A tiny breath escaped her lips. "Jack, I think I could be in love with you."

His lips curved. "Only think?"

"I'm afraid!" Embarrassed that she had blurted out her love so candidly, she started to get up. "I should have kept my mouth shut."

He clamped his hands on her shoulders to prevent her from escaping. "Even if it's something I'm glad to hear?" he asked quietly.

"It's—it's all happening so fast, Jack. The last time I followed my emotions, I married Ron, and look what happened there! Now I have two small children to consider. And—and I'm afraid," she said in a small voice.

"Of me?"

She shook her head. "Of me."

Jack looked into her eyes. "Don't be, Holly. There's a brave, beautiful woman inside you, and she's also as sharp as a tack. You *can* trust her. You and Ron were just kids when you married, and there was no way you could know for sure how he would—or wouldn't—mature. That wasn't your fault. It wasn't some flaw in your instincts. It was youth, plain and simple. But you're a grown woman now, and you've proved your instincts are sound—just look at what a fine job you've done with Caro and Ryan. Trust yourself, Holly. And trust your feelings for me." He brushed a stray curl away from her face and trailed his fingers over the curve of her cheek.

She chewed on her bottom lip. "Has anyone ever won an argument with you?"

His lips followed the path his fingers had begun. "No."

Any further words were promptly forgotten as his mouth covered hers in a breath-stealing kiss. Holly looped her arms around Jack's neck as she dropped back onto the cushion, pulling him down with her.

"You always smell like spring," he muttered, nuzzling her neck.

"You always smell like midnight," she breathed.

She gathered up the nerve to loosen his shirt and combed her fingers through the crisp curls on his chest.

"No fair."

"Why not?" she asked archly, raising her head enough to take a tentative taste of his skin, swirling her tongue around one tiny brown nipple.

"Because I can't bare your chest out here as much as I'd like to." He settled for allowing his hands to roam over the soft mounds covered by her sundress.

"Your magic has turned me into a daring woman, Sorcerer Montgomery."

He pulled back, stood up and in one move swooped her into his arms. "Then let's see how daring we both can be." He walked through the open French doors and kicked them shut behind them.

"Jack!" Holly had no choice but to keep her arms around his neck or risk falling. "You can't!"

"Can't what? Make love to you? Show you exactly how I feel and make sure you belong to me wholly?" He began climbing the stairs.

She looked up. "Can't carry me. I'm too heavy."

"Far from it. It wouldn't hurt you to gain an extra ten pounds. We'll begin with the cheesecake. Later."

Holly drew her head back to study Jack's face as he ascended. She knew if she asked him to, he'd set her back on her feet and escort her downstairs, where they would finish their wine and make small talk. Or they could end up in his bedroom, reveling in the stuff of romance novels. Except she wouldn't be relaxing in a bubble bath, reading about it happening to someone else.

When Jack reached the top of the stairs, he headed for a set of double doors left slightly ajar. He kicked them open and entered the room.

What caught Holly's attention immediately was the huge four-poster bed. She cleared her throat. "I see you have an extra-large coffin."

He slid her to her feet. "Intimidating?"

She couldn't keep her eyes off it. "Downright frightening." Then she noticed something else. The down comforter was a deep cobalt blue with splashes of pale gray. "What, no black?"

He smiled, pleased her sense of humor was overcoming her anxiety. "I told you, black was for my public image. This room is very private."

He guided her over to the bed but was clearly not pushing. He was going to let her make her own decisions. He looked down at her pensive expression, and Holly's breath slammed hard into her chest. She only hoped she could live up to his expectations.

She took a deep breath and began unbuttoning his shirt. "That day you mowed my lawn?" He arched an eyebrow. "I watched you from my living room window."

He grinned. "I know. I saw the curtains twitch."

His shirt dropped to the carpet.

She ran her fingers over his chest. "The first time you kissed my wrist, I wanted you to do more."

He reached up and pulled her hairpins out. With a smile of satisfaction curving his lips, he watched her coppery curls tumble down around her shoulders. "I thought of doing that all through lunch." He pressed his fingertips against her back. "Now all I need is a hint as to how to get you out of this lovely but very unnecessary dress."

She lifted her arms. "The zipper is on the side."

Holly experienced a moment of unease when he whisked off her dress, leaving her feeling very naked in an ecru camisole and tap pants.

"Beautiful," he breathed, gathering her up in his arms and banishing her fears.

Holly squeaked with surprise when she was lightly tossed into the middle of the large bed. Then Jack peeled off his slacks and stretched out beside her.

Laughter bubbled up in her throat. "I should have known," she said as he turned away briefly to fumble in his nightstand drawer.

"Known what?"

"That even your briefs would be black!"

But her laughter was soon silenced as he pulled her toward him and began to map out every inch of her body with his knowing fingers.

Mouth brushed across mouth, teeth nibbled tender spots, whispered endearments accompanied hotly pleasuring caresses.

Holly delighted in making Jack shudder as she rained kisses across his chest. He retaliated by peeling off her camisole and suckling her breasts, drawing on her until she felt she would explode from the pleasure. She found a tiny scar on his left thigh and kissed it better. He turned her onto her stomach and nibbled his way down her spine to the cleft in her buttocks and then began nibbling his way back up while she shivered under his ministrations.

She turned over and nipped the throbbing vein in his throat, laughing huskily when he called her his red-haired vampire and claimed that he was more under her spell than she could ever be under his.

He kept his promise of seeking out—and kissing—every single freckle . . . and every spot in between.

She mourned that her breasts were small. He showed her how perfectly they fit his hands. She thought she had no curves. He demonstrated how she curved exactly where she needed to, and how well those curves fit against his lean frame. She had thought there wasn't anything about her that could be considered sexy. He discovered her deep wells of sensuality—and tapped them.

"Give me your fire, Holly," he murmured, resting his hand against the fiery curls at the apex of her thighs. "Let me show you everything about love."

Her eyes glowed. "Yes." She couldn't stop her hips from arching under his probing touch. "Jack, please, I need you so much." She reached for him, pulling him up and over her.

Jack settled himself between her thighs, pushing slowly into her moist warmth.

Holly sighed with contentment. But contentment was quickly replaced by something more insistent burning deep within her body. Her hands fluttered against Jack's back, feeling the heat from his body, the sweat forming from his painstaking restraint in showing her just how much they could share together. But she was beyond caring about taking it slow and easy. She arched up for his thrust, eager to find the completion that hovered just beyond her reach.

"You have no idea how good you feel," he murmured, never taking his eyes from her face. "But this is only the beginning." He moved slowly, silently urging her to fly with him to that far-off pinnacle. By then they were so attuned to each other that he sensed her tiny gasp even before she uttered it, knew how close she was to climaxing. Their movements quickened, and Holly's cry of rapture was captured by Jack's hungry mouth covering hers, his own groan echoing hers.

When the last tremors began to subside and Holly felt emotions she'd never experienced well up inside her again, it was Jack who held her close to him, allowing his shoulder to soak up her tears of joy. And Jack who brushed a soft kiss across each eyelid, silently urging her to sleep until her eyes closed and she drifted off to dreams that would never again be as good as reality.

## *Chapter Fifteen*

"I'm beginning to think you like my tub more than my bed," Jack teased.

Holly laid her head back against his chest and closed her eyes. "Who wouldn't enjoy having a slave to do her bidding," she purred, "and a tub practically deep enough for swimming. Besides, long baths are my only vice."

"Only?" He bit down on her earlobe, then soothed the imaginary injury with his tongue.

Jack's fingers massaged her scalp in a delightfully stimulating shampoo.

After they'd made love again, Holly had made her way to the bathroom, only to gasp in shock at the huge marble bathtub with Jacuzzi jets. It didn't take much persuasion on Jack's part to get her into the tub. He raided Letitia's bathroom for a few feminine bath items, and while Holly sat between his legs, he leisurely scrubbed every inch of her blushing skin and shampooed her hair.

"Mmm, this is heaven," she murmured, dipping her head forward as he used a handheld shower to rinse her hair.

He then began rubbing a scented conditioner through the heavy strands.

She sniffed the subtle orange fragrance surrounding her. "Something that smells and feels this wonderful has to take out the kinks."

He nudged her. "Hey, I like your curls."

"That's only because you're not the one who has to brush them out every morning." She absently ran her hands along his thighs.

"Time to rinse," Jack warned, pressing down lightly on the back of her neck.

Holly pushed the wet hair away from her face as she turned her head. "You are a beautiful man." She lay her palm against his chest and slowly slid it downward. "And you smell beautiful."

He arched an eyebrow. "Ticia's bath oils?"

Her hand reached its destination, stroking slowly down and up.

Jack gasped in surprised pleasure. "Lady, where'd you learn to do that?"

"Books," she whispered.

"Hell, I must be writing the wrong kind."

MOST OF THEIR BATHWATER ending up splashed on the floor. They laughingly mopped up the mess, then Holly sat on a stool before the mirror while Jack carefully worked a wide-toothed comb through her tangled curls.

"This bathroom is larger than my bedroom and bath put together." Holly looked around at the extravagant fixtures.

"Hold still," he ordered amiably, working out a snag.

She looked at herself in the mirror. Her makeup was long gone, and by rights her face should have looked pale against her fiery hair. Instead her skin was flushed—from the hot bath and Jack's lovemaking—her eyes were bright, and her lips were rosy and slightly swollen. The plush black towel wrapped around her emphasized her coloring instead of draining it as the stark color usually did.

Jack draped her damp hair around her shoulders. "There."

Holly couldn't remember ever feeling so pampered, so cared for.

"How about a late-night snack?" he suggested.

"Mrs. Boggs's cheesecake?"

"Sounds good to me. You go get comfortable in the bedroom while I raid the kitchen." He put on a cotton kimono. "Ticia won't mind if you'd like to borrow something of hers."

She hesitated.

"Down the hall, third door on the right," he ordered. "And if you think my bathroom is decadent, take a look at hers."

Tucking the towel more securely around her, Holly found Letitia's room. "Wow," she murmured, looking at the delicate French furniture with soft accents of rose, blue and lavender brushed across the drapes, the silk comforter and the upholstered chairs.

The huge walk-in closet was stuffed to the gills. Holly selected a caftan, pulled it over her head and carefully closed the closet doors.

A peek into the bathroom backed up Jack's comments. The enormous, elaborate room was a sybarite's dream.

By the time Jack returned to the bedroom bearing a tray, Holly was studying the titles cramming his bookshelves.

"You look beautiful," he told her, setting the tray on the coffee table in the room's seating area.

Holly curled up on the couch and selected pieces of raw vegetables, slices of cold chicken and some left-over lobster.

"You'd better hurry if you want any food," she warned, settling back with a small plate. "I've discovered I'm very hungry."

"Must be all the exercise you've been indulging in." He swept her hair away from her nape and dropped a kiss on the soft skin.

Tingling from his touch, she said, "Yes, sir, and I suggest you eat hearty."

"Don't worry, I plan to make excellent use of our time together."

Holly thought of her children returning the next day. Part of her didn't want this magical time to end. The logical part of her knew it would have to. And then what? She pushed the question from her mind.

Jack poured wine for both of them and filled his own plate with food, settling next to her on the couch. "Ticia's planning on traveling from coast to coast in the fall," he said. "Things will be a lot quieter around here then. I'd hoped to talk her into taking her cat with her, but she claims that miserable feline has settled down here and shouldn't be parted from his new home."

The thought of Jack living in this huge house by himself made Holly feel sad. "You two are very close. I missed that when I grew up. Ivy's the closest I have to a sister."

"Yes, we've always looked out for each other. But Ticia needs to get on her own. To an extent, she's always had someone looking after her. While I enjoy having her here, I want her to realize she can rely on herself. I'm hoping her travels will do that."

Holly leaned over and put her plate on the floor, then reached to take Jack's from him. She stretched out, laying her hand on his chest, smiling when she felt his arms surround her. "Magician, stop all the clocks," she whispered. "Let time stand still for us."

He rested his cheek against her fragrant curls. "I've done just that. The clock is no longer ticking, the earth has stopped on its axis, and you're my prisoner, Holly Bennett. I will refuse to allow you to leave."

Her eyes swept over every inch of his face, cataloging the strong cheekbones, the dark brows, the equally dark eyes lit with silver lights, the proud nose and chin, the mouth that could laugh or tease or kiss her into oblivion. "Things have changed so much between us."

"And it frightens you?"

Holly didn't look away. "The future frightens me."

"I stopped time, remember?"

She shook her head. "Reality might part us for one reason or another. I might wake up and find out this was nothing more than a dream like the other one."

"What other one?"

She flushed. "At the party, you told me you hoped my fantasies would come true. That night, I dreamed I wore that green ballgown I found in your attic and danced until dawn with a man wearing a black mask. But, of course, I woke up alone. That's the difference between fantasy and reality."

Without saying a word, Jack held out his hand. Holly took it and allowed him to lead her to an assortment of packages from F.A.O. Schwarz. Looking a bit wary, he pulled out each item for her approval. Tears sprang to her eyes as she thought of the birthdays Ron had always forgotten, while this man had taken time from a hectic publicity schedule to personally shop for her children. There were beautiful books and an authentic Raggedy Ann and Andy for Caro, games and a marvelously lifelike toy sheepdog for Ryan.

"I meant it, Holly. If there's anything unsuitable here, feel free to say so," he told her.

She threw her arms around his neck and kissed him. "Thank you for thinking of them."

"There's more," he murmured, handing her a large box wrapped in copper foil.

Holly tore off the paper, lifted the lid, and separated the protective tissue paper. The green ballgown, now cleaned and mended, was carefully folded inside.

"May all your fantasies come true," Jack said quietly. "Always."

She stared at the gown. Then she dipped her head. "I—I—" Her voice came out a mere whisper. "Thank you." Her eyes gleamed with moisture.

He stood behind her, his arms wrapped around her body in an embrace that was both comforting and arousing. "Enjoy it."

Holly put down the package and led him to the bed. "I'd much rather enjoy you," she said shyly. "If you care to protest, I suggest you do it now."

"Not on your life!"

THE NEXT MORNING, as they lazed in bed, Jack picked up her hand, running his fingertips across her knuckles and turning her hand over to trace the lines in her palm before dropping a kiss in the center. "Have you given any serious thought to having your own business?" He traced her lifeline back and forth in a featherlight motion that sent tingles up Holly's arm.

"Some. It would mean a lot of hard work in the beginning, but it's tempting," she admitted. "Still, it's a scary proposition. You need capital, and so many businesses fail within the first year."

Now he worked on her love line. "I don't think you'd be one of those."

She twisted in his arms, resting her cheek in the hollow of his shoulder. "Well, then, Master Magician, what will you do? Wave your wand and make Celia disappear?"

"If I could, I would."

The faint sounds of car doors slamming and voices from below intruded into their private world. Jack swore under his breath.

"The clocks have begun ticking again," Holly murmured sorrowfully. She pushed herself from his embrace. "I have to get dressed." She stood up and looked around.

Jack pulled on a pair of cotton shorts. "I hung your dress in the closet," he told her. "Go ahead and do whatever you need to do. I'll keep them occupied."

"They're going to know I didn't just show up here today."

He grasped her shoulders and swung her around to face him. When she kept her head down, he gripped her chin and forced it upward. "Does it bother you so much that Ivy and Letitia will know you spent the night here?"

"It's not something I make a habit of."

"A good thing you don't, my love. I've discovered I have a very possessive streak where you're concerned." He pulled her to him for a lingering kiss. "Maybe I could simply lock you away in this room."

"We have to let the world in sometime," she said softly.

His mouth brushed across hers, once, twice. But the front door had just slammed shut, and he could hear voices echoing in the high-ceilinged entryway. He swore again.

"Too bad they couldn't have been delayed," he muttered, reluctantly releasing her. "I'll go down and give you some time. Now, I've got to get out of here before I give in to my baser instincts." He quickly left the bedroom, carefully closing the doors behind him.

Holly looked around the room where she had spent some of her happiest hours. Then she began dressing to face reality again.

"THERE YOU ARE," Letitia called out from the den. "Why, Jack, you look tired. Did something interfere with your beauty rest while we were gone?" she said coyly.

He shot her a look. "Stuff it, Ticia."

"I saw Holly's car outside," Ivy said.

"Where's Mom?" Ryan demanded, hopping from one foot to the other. "We've got so much to tell her."

"She's upstairs freshening up," Jack explained, picking Ryan up. "She'll be down in a minute. How was Vermont?"

"Terence Blake was drop-dead gorgeous and spent hours discussing obscure books with Ivy while the children and I communed with nature." Letitia absently scratched her arm.

"She got poison oak," Ryan told Jack. "Caro and I told her not to go near those leaves, but she didn't listen to us. Mr. Blake had calamine lotion and yellow soap, but Ticia's still been itchin' like a dog with fleas."

Letitia grimaced. "Oh, please, Ryan, that's a horrible way to describe my misery!"

"What did you do with Holly, lock her in a closet?" Ivy asked.

"Lock who in a closet?" Holly appeared in the doorway.

"Mom!" Both children ran to her, wrapping their arms around her legs, talking a mile a minute.

"Slow down. One at a time," she laughed. "I gather you had fun."

"Mr. Blake had a barn and chickens and ducks and kittens and puppies and a pond that I fell in," Ryan confided. "But Ticia fished me out. And we were both all green and slimy!" He grinned. "Then Ticia got poison oak, and she's been scratchin' all the time."

Letitia groaned. "Isn't it amazing what some people consider entertaining?"

"Did you miss us?" Caro asked.

"Naturally." Holly gave her a big hug and dropped a kiss on her forehead.

"What'd you do while we were gone?" Ryan asked.

The silence was deafening. Ivy and Letitia leaned forward, eagerly awaiting her reply.

"I spent some time with Jack, and we just... puttered around."

"That's a new way of describing it," Letitia murmured.

"Chicken," Ivy muttered under her breath, sidling up to Holly. "I want to hear all the details later."

Holly smiled. "In your dreams."

"That's probably the closest I'll ever get." Ivy tossed her car keys up and down in her hand. "Kids, why don't you drive back into town with me? We'll stop for ice cream."

Ryan whooped his assent, while Caro hesitated. "Maybe Mom would like us to stay with her," she whispered.

Holly glanced at Jack, grateful to see his smile of understanding. "I would love it," she assured her daughter. "But I'll be leaving very soon, too. If you guys stop for ice cream, I might even be home before you get there. Then you can tell me all about your weekend."

"Then we could help Aunt Ivy unload the car," Caro decided.

"That's help I won't turn down," Ivy told her.

"Are you and Jack real good friends now?" Ryan questioned.

She was cautious. "Yes, I'd say so."

"Great!" He jumped up in the air. "Then you'll fall in love and get married, and we'll have a real dad and I can have my puppy! Kevin's magic spell worked, just like he said it would."

Holly gazed at the frozen tableau before her. Jack looked a bit uneasy, Ivy looked everywhere but at her, and Letitia murmured something about looking for her cat.

"Am I missing something here?" Holly asked, looking from one to the other.

"Don't be mad at us," Ryan begged. "Kevin said he could make us a dad from magic, and he did. He made Jack. We know because we were there when Jack came out of the fog that night. And now you two are friends, so you can get married. We paid three dollars for him, too."

"Time to go," Ivy said with false cheerfulness, ushering the children out the door. "We want to make it to the ice cream parlor before it closes."

Holly felt her horror rise. She wanted some answers, right now. "Wait a minute!"

Ivy ignored her summons and practically stampeded the two children out to her car. Holly spun around and found Jack standing in the doorway with his hands jammed in his shorts pockets. Letitia had conveniently disappeared.

"You know what's going on."

He nodded. "Let's go into the den."

"Let's not." A few things that had kept hammering in her mind finally fell into place. "It's becoming clear now. Why Ryan kept insisting Kevin owed him money, and why Ryan and Caro came out here to see you when supposedly they didn't know you. They thought you were the result of their magic spell." She found it increasingly difficult to breathe. Her voice rose with her agitation. "No wonder Ivy was convinced Kevin had stolen her book of spells. He had!"

He held out his hand. "Holly, you're making too much of this."

She wasn't sure whether to laugh or cry at the idea her children were convinced Jack was created by magic just for her. "Then you clear it up for me."

Without suggesting they adjourn to another room, Jack succinctly began with what he'd overheard the night of summer solstice, what he'd later learned, and how easy it was for the children to believe he was magic, considering his sudden presence in the fog just after Kevin had uttered the spell.

"They actually thought they could use witchcraft to get me a husband?" She was incredulous.

"Yes, and if I were you, I'd be flattered that they loved you that much."

Holly wasn't sure if it was flattery or horror that kept her frozen to the spot. "Is that why you were so insistent I be the one to look at the clothing in the attic? Because of my children?"

"In the beginning my curiosity was piqued about a woman who could inspire such love in her children," he said without hesitation. "The same woman ultimately inspired love in me."

Holly was lost in wavering emotions. "The secrets, the whispered conversations, all the talk of magic..." She still wasn't sure who to believe. "I should paddle their behinds for going out to the meadow so late at night and for accepting a ride with a stranger. Not to mention being accessories to Kevin's theft!" A tiny burst of hysterical laughter worked its way up her throat. "I can't believe they thought chanting a few words and using a few pictures would conjure up a man for me to fall in love with."

"It appears to have worked," he quietly pointed out.

Holly sighed deeply, and finally her lips curved upward. "It appears we're under a magic spell, after all, M[illegible]ter Magician. The only difference is, it wasn't one
ur making." She shook her head. "To think even
ems to have known about this! I want to see

what she has to say for herself. I guess I'd better get on home before the kids do."

He took her in his arms. "All right. You go on home and see to the kids. But how about all of us going out to dinner tomorrow night?"

"Sounds wonderful. Unless the kids try another spell and make one of us disappear," she said wryly.

Their kiss was all too brief before Jack walked Holly out to her car.

"I have to give them credit." She looked up at him through the open car window.

"Why?"

Holly grinned mischievously. "At least they had excellent taste. I could have ended up with Mister Rogers or the Cookie Monster!" With a wag of her fingers, she drove off.

"Now that you've compromised the lady, are you going to make an honest woman of her?" Letitia asked from the open door.

"As soon as we both get used to each other, I intend to propose. Any problem with that?"

"None whatsoever. In fact, I wouldn't be surprised if you suddenly decided to change your writing hours to days only, so you can devote your nights to other pursuits." Her amused laughter floated after her as she walked back into the house.

"I can't wait to meet the man to take you on," Jack muttered, following her inside.

## *Chapter Sixteen*

"I'm six," Ryan announced to one and all. "I can go to a *real* school now. No baby schools for me." He pointed to his chest.

Holly rolled her eyes.

"Hey, this is an important day for him," Jack chided. "Let him brag."

"You weren't the one who was awakened at dawn by his trooping up and down the hallway screaming at the top of his lungs, 'Six, six, six!'" she said wryly, setting paper plates out on the picnic table.

Jack watched Ivy organize eight six-year-olds in a game under a stand of trees. Kevin stood off to one side, alternating between keeping the kids in line and watching Jack with narrowed eyes.

"I'm still under observation," he commented out of the corner of his mouth.

"At least he's finally stopped putting garlic on everything." She laughed and handed him a jug of punch and some paper cups. "Here, you're not going to get out of your share of the work. Pour only half a cup at a time for them. They can always ask for more. That way they're less likely to spill on each other."

As she set out Ryan's birthday cake, Holly watched Jack out of the corner of her eye, still marveling at his presence in her life. The summer was almost gone, Labor Day just around the corner, and Jack's publicity touring had begun in earnest, taking the edge off the werewolf-warlock theories of his existence. Now the local gossips focused on his romance with Holly Bennett. A horror novelist living in a haunted house in Salem was juicy; that the woman he was seeing was the descendant of a convicted witch was even better.

In the space of one summer life had changed so much. Holly watched Caro and Ryan becoming more independent each day. She saw the beginning of a new romance for Ivy with a gentleman from Vermont. And with each passing day, she fell more in love with Jack.

"Don't those little darlings realize how hot it is?" Letitia collapsed on a picnic bench, picked up a paper cup and drank thirstily. She wrinkled her nose with distaste. "They actually drink this stuff?"

"It would be worse if I hadn't gotten the sugar-free punch," Holly replied, putting out colorful clown napkins. "A horde of kids running around on a sugar high is downright scary."

Letitia shook her head in wonderment.

"Changing your mind about having a baby?" Jack teased.

"Of course not. One of these days I fully intend to contact a sperm bank," she said haughtily.

Holly chuckled at the running joke.

"Don't you have a date with that attorney tonight?" Jack asked his sister.

She shook her head. "I told him I had a birthday celebration to attend. He acted as if he hoped he'd be invited—probably thought it was some society do. I decided to leave him guessing," she giggled.

"At this rate, you're going to run out of eligible men within a month," Holly said, steadying the centerpiece of helium balloons attached to a battleship Jack had given Ryan. "What happened to that real estate broker you dated?"

"He had the mistaken idea dinner out included my going to bed with him," she said bluntly.

"She sicced Le Chat on him. He was allergic to cats," Jack pointed out. "Think it's time to rescue Ivy and feed the horde?"

Holly didn't have to call out twice. The rest of the afternoon passed quickly as the kids demolished cake, ice cream and punch in record time. Ryan opened his gifts, and they finally chauffeured the children to their homes, finishing off the day with Ryan's requested pizza and video games.

"This is the best birthday I've ever had," Ryan decided, wiping pizza sauce from his mouth. He looked across the table at Jack, who sat next to Holly. "You were worth the three dollars Caro and I gave Kevin for the spell."

"Aw, jeez, Ryan, give it a rest," Kevin groaned. "I had to mow old Mrs. Timmons's lawn all summer because of that."

"And you'll be shoveling her walks all winter, too," Ivy cooed.

"Why not just ask me to kill myself while you're at it?"

"Because that would be much too easy."

"Ryan, we discussed the spell and how it wasn't real," Holly reminded him. "And you told me you understood."

"Yeah, I know there aren't witches and ghosts and stuff. But Aunt Ivy's books are real, so I decided that maybe this time the spell had to be real," he said logically.

Holly threw her hands up in defeat.

"Let's hit the video games," Jack suggested to the three children, who jumped at the chance.

"That man is perfect father material," Ivy declared, turning to Holly. "So why aren't you doing something about it?"

"Oh, Ivy, there's so much going on right now, between his working on his new manuscript and doing publicity for his other books. He's also been invited to speak at a writer's convention next month. And then there's his proposal for his new series."

"A series of books?" Ivy poured more punch from the pitcher. "What about?"

Holly shrugged. "He won't talk about them. Said he's superstitious that way. He did say that once he has the first book roughed out he wants me to read it. Has he mentioned it to you, Ticia?"

Letitia concentrated on picking olives off her slice of pizza. "Not really. He just holes up in his office all night and types his fingers to the bone."

Holly frowned. Did Letitia know something she didn't?

THAT EVENING HOLLY PUT a tired Caro and Ryan to bed and returned to the living room, where Jack had tall glasses of iced tea waiting.

"For a while I wasn't sure I could get them to settle down." She sighed, collapsing on the couch beside him.

"Ryan turned six today—a milestone." He handed her a glass.

She sipped the cold liquid gratefully. "I shudder to think of six*teen,* when he can go for his driver's license." She curled her legs under her and leaned against Jack, resting her head on his shoulder. "How's your writing going?"

"It's coming together. Funny how I used to prefer writing all night. Now I'd much rather spend my nights indulging in other activities." He playfully nipped her ear.

"I can't wait to read it. Ivy asked what the series was about, but I explained your superstition." Did she imagine his slight stiffening? "You won't even give me a hint about it?"

"I set it locally."

"Anything else?" she wheedled.

"I don't snore."

She smirked. "I already know that."

"I can't imagine how, since I don't do a hell of a lot of sleeping when you're with me." He nibbled his way across her collarbone. "Mmm, you always taste so good. Thank heaven Ivy's been good enough to take Ryan and Caro with her every time she drives up to see her friend in Vermont."

"With school starting soon, they won't be able to go up as much," she murmured, twisting her body around.

"There're other ways. The kids already have their rooms picked out at my house," he reminded her.

"Oh, Jack, I don't know about that. They've been hurt enough. I can't set them up for that again."

"I'm not Ron," he growled, his features darkening with anger. "I don't intend to abandon you for some overdeveloped teenager. I love you, and you love me. What else is there?''

''You still keep secrets,'' she complained, levering away from him. ''Ticia knows about your new series of books, doesn't she? You say you love me, but you won't tell me. Why not?''

''She only knows because she has a nasty habit of entering my office uninvited and reading over my shoulder nights she can't sleep,'' he retorted.

Holly clamped her lips shut. ''I can't handle secrets.''

Jack withdrew. ''What you really mean is you don't trust me.''

''I . . . I trust you. I just don't like things being kept from me.''

He took a deep breath. ''Is there a reason you're trying to pick a fight?''

''I don't want to argue. I just don't want to be lied to.''

He pulled her into his arms. ''Holly, I love you so much, I hate to be away from you. I want us to live in the same house, be together all the time. Let me be Caro and Ryan's father. Let us banish all the ghosts of the past.''

Holly wanted to say yes so badly, but something stayed her tongue. ''You have that television interview in Los Angeles next week,'' she said softly, looking down. ''I'll give you my answer when you get back.''

His dark eyes gleamed. ''The answer I want?''

''I have an idea you wouldn't accept any other,'' she said dryly.

''Then can we forget our argument and get down to some serious necking?''

She linked her arms around his neck. She told herself he wasn't keeping anything important from her and she shouldn't be so sensitive. Jack would never betray her the way Ron had. "I don't see why not."

"WHEN ARE YOU GOING to put that man out of his misery and marry him?" Ivy asked as she and Holly shared lunch in the back of the clothing shop.

"When he returns from Los Angeles." Holly swirled her spoon through a container of raspberry yogurt. "Ticia's taping the talk show, and I'm going over tonight to watch it. He'll be home tomorrow."

Ivy smiled. "You deserve all the good luck you've gotten," she said. "Has Celia recovered from Jack's donating the antique clothing to the museum?"

She shook her head. "She claims he did it out of spite. Speaking of men, though, what about Terence Blake? You've been seeing him almost every weekend. Do you think anything will come of it?"

Ivy shrugged. "To be perfectly honest, I don't know. I'm such a people person, and he's such a recluse. He's perfectly happy doing his financial consultant work by computer, telephone and modem." She looked pensive for a moment. "Only time will tell. Oh, you'll never guess what I heard!" She leaned forward. "Eileen Butkus is pregnant. She saw Dr. Sawyer yesterday and threw a royal tantrum in his office when he confirmed her worst fears."

"Ron claims he didn't want the first two. What will he do with a third?" Holly asked wryly.

Ivy shook her head. "That's just it. Word has it she gave him the news last night, and he cleared out before dawn. I figured you'd rather hear the news from me than from the grapevine."

"You're right. I'm just surprised Sally Adams wasn't in here first thing to tell me all the gory details." She tossed her yogurt container into the trash. "Ron's the one who's ended up the loser in all this. He'll just keep running until there's no new place to run." Holly shrugged. "I feel sorry for Eileen, though. She's become another one of his victims."

"I wouldn't worry about her. She's the type to land on her feet." Ivy rose. "Well, back to the salt mines."

DINNER WAS A QUICK AFFAIR in the Bennett household before they drove out to Jack's house to see his interview.

"When are we gonna live in Jack's house?" Ryan asked as they climbed out of the car.

Holly smiled at him. "Would you like to?"

"Yes! Then we could have a puppy!" he shouted.

"I am so sick of this puppy stuff," Caroline groaned. "Mom, can't you make him stop?" She punched her brother in the arm.

"Both of you, stop it," Holly ordered, walking up the steps to the front door.

Letitia pulled it open and greeted them with a warm smile. "I was in Boston all day, so I haven't had a chance to see it, either," she explained as they walked into the den. "Jack left a message on the answering machine that it wasn't one of his best interviews. He said more, but there was static on the line, so I couldn't understand him." She picked up the remote control and turned on the television and VCR, fast-forwarding the tape until they saw Jack's face.

"Look at that woman practically drool over him," Letitia said with disgust as the interviewer introduced

Jack with a list of his published books and an excerpt from his latest novel.

"I understand you're working on a series of books set in your new home of Salem, Massachusetts." The woman flashed Jack a toothy smile.

He shifted in his chair. "That's right."

"Yet you haven't said any more than that," she went on. He ignored her hint. "Mr. Montgomery, you've already gained a new legion of fans. Surely you want to whet their appetites for your work in progress."

"Not really. The first book won't be published for about eighteen months. They can find out then," he said, tight-lipped.

The woman's smile grew broader. "Ah, but I was able to learn something about this new series," she announced, smiling confidentially at her audience as if she was about to reveal a state secret. "I was able to find out that not only is it set in Salem, but the main character is a woman burned at the stake during the witchcraft trials. She places a curse on a prominent family and comes back every generation to seduce the oldest son and eventually destroy him. There's talk that the curse will be broken in the last book, when true love will enter the picture."

Holly sat frozen in her chair, bitter nausea rising in her throat.

Jack looked as if he was exerting a great deal of willpower to hold on to his temper. "I have no idea where you heard that," he bit out.

"I have my sources." She laughed musically. "Now please tell us more about this new series. It sounds fascinating."

He looked like a dark avenging angel. "No," he said firmly, the kiss of death for an interview. The show went downhill from there as the woman grappled, to no avail, to draw out her now grave and wholly uncooperative subject.

"No wonder he wouldn't tell me about it," Holly whispered, slowly rising to her feet.

"Holly, it isn't what you think," Letitia said.

"Isn't it?" She left the room and went upstairs. There was only one place where she could find the truth, and that was in Jack's office. Grateful he'd once shown her how to use his computer, she quickly searched through the disks until she found the one she wanted.

"I didn't want you to find out this way."

She spun around, her body stiff with pain from learning she'd been duped once again. "I thought you weren't due home until tomorrow," she said coldly.

Jack entered the room and closed the door behind him, leaning against the heavy wood. "I took an earlier flight. After that damn interview, I knew I had to get back here as soon as possible."

She felt a crushing blow in the vicinity of her heart. "You were so curious about Priscilla, and despite my objections, you used her as a subject for your proposal. How fitting. Since evidently you were using me, too."

"I never used you, Holly. You know that."

"Then why wouldn't you tell me about your book?" she demanded, refusing to give in to her tears in front of him.

"Because you were so sensitive about Priscilla. I wanted you to read my treatment of the subject before you closed your mind entirely to the possibilities."

She gulped. "You said you'd never betray me or hurt me, but you have."

His eyes were bleak. "Holly, I think you'd be pleased with how I've handled it."

She was beyond hearing. All she knew was that she couldn't breathe for the constriction in her chest. Pain flowed over her in waves. "What else haven't you told me? What other secrets have you kept?"

Her pain was mirrored on his face. "There are no other secrets, Holly."

"My children conjuring you up with a magic spell? Wasn't that a secret? The fact that you had no intention of selling those clothes to Celia? Shall I go on?" Her chest heaved. "I have to get out of here." She tried to push her way past him.

He reached for her but halted when she flinched. "We need to talk, Holly."

She shook her head. "No, I think there's been enough talk. Right now, I feel used. I need to be alone and do some thinking."

"I'll call you tomorrow."

"No!" She fought to keep her voice from trembling. "I don't want to hear from you, Jack. Not until I sort all this out. What is it they say? 'Don't call me, I'll call you.' That's what I want." She opened the door and quickly walked out, closing it behind her with a final-sounding click.

Jack swore fiercely under his breath.

Letitia hurried into the room. "It was a shock. She'll be all right once she's thought things through," she assured her brother.

He slumped in his chair. "Will she?"

Letitia went to his side and crouched down beside him. "Jack, Holly loves you very much. She isn't going to throw that away."

He blinked rapidly against the moisture gathering in his eyes. Raw pain clawed at his insides.

"I have to give her time. It's going to kill me, but I have to."

Letitia touched his hand. "I'll put in a good word for you."

He shook his head. "No, it has to be up to Holly. But it hurts, Ticia. It really hurts."

She put her arms around her brother, and, for the first time, Letitia had nothing to say.

## *Chapter Seventeen*

"Holly, you can't hide out forever."

She tried to summon up a smile for Ivy but failed miserably. "I'm not hiding out."

"You are if you're insisting you aren't going to Aunt Prudence and Aunt Patience's costume ball," she pointed out. "You haven't missed one since the year we were old enough to attend. Kevin already promised to take Caro and Ryan trick-or-treating in the neighborhood, then on to the slumber party at the Andersons'. You won't have to worry about them until morning."

Holly picked at a snag in her sweater. She couldn't find the enthusiasm for much of anything lately. "I drove by the house today. It's still empty."

When she had told Jack she needed to think things over, she hadn't expected him to pack up and leave. Mrs. Boggs only said she was paid to keep the place clean while Mr. Montgomery and his sister did some traveling. Every time someone asked her if she'd heard from Jack, she felt another slice cut out of her heart. Keeping a smile pasted on her lips had been a massive chore for the past two months.

Ivy touched her shoulder. "Personally, I would think it would be easier for you with him gone."

She dropped onto the couch. "I did it again. I overreacted and lashed out at him. I hurt him because I was hurting. I felt used because of the story he was going to write." She glanced at a box that lay on the coffee table. "I received that yesterday from his agent. It's a copy of the manuscript. I stayed up all night reading it, Ivy. It's very good. He more than did justice to his Priscilla Drake character," she whispered. "The novel is deep and thought-provoking and wonderful."

"What are you going to do?"

"I don't know." Holly looked plain miserable. "I thought of sending a message back to him through his agent, but I can't seem to get up the nerve." She choked back a slightly hysterical sob. "My car hasn't been the same since he's been gone, Celia's sold the shop, so I'm out of a job, the dentist said Caro's new teeth are coming in crooked and she'll eventually need braces. I can't sleep. I can't work. I can't do anything because I did something stupid and I can't make it right!"

Ivy perched on the couch and placed an arm around her friend's shoulder. "Holly, it's Halloween, the night we people of Salem revere," she said softly. "You need to get out, see other people. Caro and Ryan tiptoe around you as if afraid you'll break if they say one wrong word. Ryan confessed the last time he asked you about Jack, you broke down and cried. He's afraid to even say his name. Caro looks just as miserable as you do. You have to snap out of it."

Holly's face was downcast as she picked at the hole in her jeans. "I drive men away, Ivy. I drove Ron away, and I drove Jack away."

"You did no such thing!" Ivy snapped, standing up. "Now go upstairs and get dressed for the ball before I do something violent to you!"

"I can't."

"You can." Ivy grabbed her hand and pulled her to her feet. "You're going if I have to dress you myself and drag you there."

Holly should have realized the error of letting Ivy look through her closet. The moment she pulled out the green ballgown, Holly felt the tears brim.

"None of that," Ivy ordered. "Now, into the dress. Don't you have combs to go with the dress?" She rummaged through Holly's drawers until she found them and a silk half mask.

"Ivy, I can't wear it!" she almost wailed.

"Yes, you can. And you're going to dance and drink champagne and have the time of your life."

"If you don't smile, people will think you were dragged here against your will," Ivy muttered as they entered the Tutweiler ballroom.

"I *was* dragged here against my will."

Ivy grabbed two glasses of champagne and handed one to Holly. "Men are looking at you as if you were a rich dessert. Women envy you your gown. Relish tonight, Cinderella."

Holly's laugh held no humor. "Cinderella? Wrong story, Ivy. She attended a ball and met a prince."

"Will I do?"

That old tingling sensation danced along the back of Holly's neck. She slowly turned and found a tall man dressed in black evening wear of the same era as her gown.

"May I have this dance?" He held out a hand.

Stunned, unable to think of a coherent reply, she silently gave him her hand and allowed him to lead her onto the dance floor. From the moment the strains of a waltz were struck up, Holly felt as if she was reliving her dream. Except this time she was awake and knew the identity of her dance partner.

"You came back," she whispered.

"I had to. I left something very important behind."

"I received a package from your agent."

"I asked her to send it to you."

"It was very good. You were right." She was past caring whether she was making sense. All she wanted to do was drink in his nearness. *Where have you been? Why did you leave? You're so thin. I love you!* ran through her mind, but she couldn't find a way to say any of it out loud.

His half mask hid enough of his face to cover any expression that would help Holly gauge his feelings.

"Is Letitia here?" she asked.

"No, she's taking her time driving cross-country."

Jack didn't say another word as the dance ended. People crowded around him, asking about his trip, if he was back to stay, about his new books.

"You knew he was going to be here, didn't you?" Holly cornered Ivy much later in the evening.

"No, I didn't."

Holly searched her friend's face and saw that she spoke the truth. "But?"

Ivy leaned over and whispered in her ear. "Aunt Prudence said she knew Jack would be here and that you would be wearing a green gown."

Holly's eyes widened. "You mean Jack called her and said he'd be here."

Ivy shook her head. She looked just as confused as Holly.

Holly's brow creased in a frown. "Then how did she know?"

"Maybe Aunt Pru finally got a prediction right. Either way, enjoy it, kiddo. And don't blow it!" She patted her shoulder and moved off.

The evening was rapidly disappearing. What would happen when the ball was over? Would Jack leave again?

He suddenly appeared with her cape tossed over his arm.

"I'll drive you home," he announced, leaving no room for argument.

Holly was tucked into the sleek black car. Jack remained silent during the drive. He parked in her driveway and escorted her to the door. For a moment she feared he was going to leave her before she could get out the words she needed to say, but he only held out his hand for her key and opened the door, following her inside.

She licked suddenly dry lips. "Would you like some wine or coffee?"

He shook his head. "We need to talk, Holly."

She sank onto the couch, the skirt of her gown billowing around her as he sat down on the chair facing her.

"I've made a lot of mistakes in my life," Jack said quietly, looking down at his laced hands. "The biggest one had to do with you."

Holly felt as if her heart had lodged in her throat.

"I shouldn't have left before we tried to work things out. You were hurting that night, and so was I. I knew you needed time, and I was afraid if I didn't get away, I would storm your house, pressure you, and probably make things worse. I didn't want that to happen, so I borrowed my agent's cabin in New Hampshire and finished my book."

She licked her dry lips. "It didn't take me long to realize how foolish I'd been. You're nothing like Ron. And I guess I've been so sensitive about Priscilla all my life. Maybe because she'd seemed like just another helpless victim. Except by the time I worked up the nerve to tell you, you were already gone." She lifted her head, displaying emerald eyes glistening with unshed tears. "I thought I'd lost you forever. And it was all my fault."

Jack leaned forward and clasped her hands between his. "You weren't going to lose me," he assured her. "I just wanted to give you the time you needed. All I did up there was pace the floor and think about you. Think about loving you." A smile touched his lips. "And think about watching Ryan play Little League and attending Caro's first ballet recital."

The tears now streamed freely down her cheeks. "Are you sure?"

His gaze bored into hers. "I always have been. You said you'd give me an answer when I returned from L.A. It's a little late, but do you think I could have it now?"

"Yes," she whispered.

Jack exhaled a deep breath. "I can't handle a long engagement," he warned.

"I don't think I can, either," she confessed.

He stood up and pulled her to her feet. "Where are the kids?" He buried his face against her hair.

"At a neighbor's for a Halloween slumber party," she mumbled against his shirtfront.

His eyes twinkled with unholy lights. "Then we have the house to ourselves?"

"All night."

"Think they'll mind finding me here tomorrow?"

She touched his face in a tender caress. "They'll be ecstatic. They've missed you almost as much as I have. At first, Ryan was afraid the magic spell had backfired, sending you back into some awful netherworld. Kevin felt so bad he even gave back the three dollars."

"That kid is turning around."

She rested her cheek against his. "Let's not talk about Kevin."

"Fine with me. We have far more important things to discuss. Such as our wedding, what kind of puppy to get, whether you'll mind running your own shop." She pulled back to look at him. "I'm the one who bought Celia's shop," he confessed. "Of course, you'll have to change the name."

She was stunned. "But—"

"No buts," he said firmly.

Something else occurred to her. "Jack, did you call Aunt Prudence or Aunt Patience and tell them you were coming to the ball?"

He shook his head. "I took a chance you'd be there. That you were wearing the gown was more than I'd dare hope for. Why do you ask?"

Her smile was a ray of sunshine. "No reason. I was just curious."

He swooped her up into his arms and climbed the stairs, easily negotiating the narrow hallway.

When they reached her bedroom he placed her on her feet, groaning at the gown's dozens of hooks. He tackled the task with manly determination. As he pulled back the bedcovers for her, he looked over his shoulder and flashed a wicked grin.

"Lady, you're in for a treat. Just for you, I'm wearing fire-engine-red briefs. I figure if anyone can wean me away from black, it's you."

Holly held her hands tightly in front of her. "This isn't another dream, is it, Jack?" she asked breathlessly, a tiny bit of fear in her eyes. "You're not going to disappear in a puff of smoke, are you?"

He stroked his palms from her wrists up to her bare shoulders. "Honey, we've got magic on our side, remember? This is a dream that will last a lifetime."

**OFFICIAL RULES • MILLION DOLLAR WISHBOOK SWEEPSTAKES**
NO PURCHASE OR OBLIGATION NECESSARY TO ENTER

To enter, follow the directions published. If the Wishbook Game Card is missing, hand-print your name and address on a 3" ×5" card and mail to either: Harlequin Wishbook, 3010 Walden Ave., P.O. Box 1867, Buffalo, NY 14269-1867, or Harlequin Wishbook, P.O. Box 609, Fort Erie, Ontario L2A 5X3, and upon receipt of your entry we will assign you Sweepstakes numbers (Limit: one entry per envelope). For eligibility, entries must be received no later than March 31, 1994 and be sent via 1st-class mail. No liability is assumed for printing errors or lost, late or misdirected entries.

To determine winners, the Sweepstakes numbers on submitted entries will be compared against a list of randomly, pre-selected prizewinning numbers. In the event all prizes are not claimed via the return of prizewinning numbers, random drawings will be held from among all other entries received to award unclaimed prizes.

Prizewinners will be determined no later than May 30, 1994. Selection of winning numbers and random drawings are under the supervision of D.L. Blair, Inc., an independent judging organization whose decisions are final. One prize to a family or organization. No substitution will be made for any prize, except as offered. Taxes and duties on all prizes are the sole responsibility of winners. Winners will be notified by mail. Chances of winning are determined by the number of entries distributed and received.

Sweepstakes open to persons 18 years of age or older, except employees and immediate family members of Torstar Corporation, D.L. Blair, Inc., their affiliates, subsidiaries and all other agencies, entities and persons connected with the use, marketing or conduct of this Sweepstakes. All applicable laws and regulations apply. Sweepstakes offer void wherever prohibited by law. Any litigation within the province of Quebec respecting the conduct and awarding of a prize in this Sweepstakes must be submitted to the Régies des Loteries et Courses du Quebec. In order to win a prize, residents of Canada will be required to correctly answer a time-limited arithmetical skill-testing question. Values of all prizes are in U.S. currency.

Winners of major prizes will be obligated to sign and return an affidavit of eligibility and release of liability within 30 days of notification. In the event of non-compliance within this time period, prize may be awarded to an alternate winner. Any prize or prize notification returned as undeliverable will result in the awarding of the prize to an alternate winner. By acceptance of their prize, winners consent to use of their names, photographs or other likenesses for purposes of advertising, trade and promotion on behalf of Torstar Corporation without further compensation, unless prohibited by law.

This Sweepstakes is presented by Torstar Corporation, its subsidiaries and affiliates in conjunction with book, merchandise and/or product offerings. Prizes are as follows: Grand Prize—$1,000,000 (payable at $33,333.33 a year for 30 years). First through Sixth Prizes may be presented in different creative executions, each with the following approximate values: First Prize—$35,000; Second Prize—$10,000; 2 Third Prizes—$5,000 each; 5 Fourth Prizes—$1,000 each; 10 Fifth Prizes—$250 each; 1,000 Sixth Prizes—$100 each. Prizewinners will have the opportunity of selecting any prize offered for that level. A travel-prize option if offered and selected by winner, must be completed within 12 months of selection and is subject to hotel and flight accommodations availability. Torstar Corporation may present this Sweepstakes utilizing names other than Million Dollar Sweepstakes. For a current list of all prize options offered within prize levels and all names the Sweepstakes may utilize, send a self-addressed stamped envelope (WA residents need not affix return postage) to: Million Dollar Sweepstakes Prize Options/Names, P.O. Box 4710, Blair, NE 68009.

For a list of prizewinners (available after July 31, 1994) send a separate, stamped self-addressed envelope to: Million Dollar Sweepstakes Winners, P.O. Box 4728, Blair NE 68009.

The Extra Bonus Prize will be awarded in a random drawing to be conducted no later than 5/30/94 from among all entries received. To qualify, entries must be received by 3/31/94 and comply with published directions. No purchase necessary. For complete rules, send a self-addressed, stamped envelope (WA residents need not affix return postage) to: Extra Bonus Prize Rules, P.O. Box 4600, Blair, NE 68009.

SW9-92